The Alpha Plague 7

Michael Robertson

Website and Newsletter:
www.michaelrobertson.co.uk

Email: subscribers@michaelrobertson.co.uk

Edited by:
Terri King - http://terri-king.wix.com/editing
And
Pauline Nolet - http://www.paulinenolet.com

Cover Design by Christian Bentulan

Formatting by Polgarus Studio

The Alpha Plague 7
Michael Robertson
© 2017 Michael Robertson

Would you like to be notified when The Alpha Plague 8 becomes available? Join my mailing list for all of my updates here:-

www.michaelrobertson.co.uk

Prologue

The letter shook in Flynn's hand as he stared down at Vicky's untidy handwriting. How could she leave him there on his own? Most days she wouldn't let him walk around Home without breathing down his neck. It didn't make sense. Or maybe he didn't want to believe it made sense. Maybe he'd driven her away with his behaviour. He hadn't exactly been kind to her.

When Flynn stood up, he wobbled on his tired legs, the effects of sleep still with him. He bent down to pick his shoes up and stumbled when he tried to put one of them on. To prevent himself from falling over, he pressed his right hand against the wall, crushing Vicky's letter against it in the process.

After he'd slipped both of his shoes on, Flynn walked out of his room, leaving the door open behind him.

The sound of the people in the canteen came at Flynn as he walked up the corridor. A wash of noise, the collective hum of conversation made each word spoken utterly indecipherable.

Maybe all the people in the place had turned up for breakfast. Hard to tell because it somehow sounded much quieter than usual—not surprising considering how many had died on the battlefield. But had anyone other than Vicky decided to leave?

Flynn entered the canteen, stopped, and looked at the diners. It already seemed like a waste of time. Although, as the communal area in the building, it had been the obvious place to come to. Maybe Vicky would still be there, and he could catch her before she left. She might have even changed her mind.

Flynn looked at all the people eating. So few compared to what had been there before they went to war. An ache tugged on his throat and he swallowed it down; he couldn't see Vicky. He'd been an idiot to think he might have.

Although they talked, many people ate with bowed heads while the screens on the far wall showed the scores of diseased outside. It would be a while before they didn't.

If Flynn looked hard enough, he'd undoubtedly see people he knew in the diseased horde. He didn't feel ready for that, and by the look of the people in the canteen, no one else did either.

It took for Flynn to look down at the letter in his hand to see he'd crushed it completely in his balled fist. He clenched his jaw and breathed through his nose, inhaling the smell of boiled cabbage that accompanied every meal. What a moron he was to think Vicky would have changed her mind.

Although he looked over the place, nobody looked up. Most seemed too lost in their own grief; everybody had lost someone. Then Brian lifted his head.

Maybe Flynn should have stayed in his room, but now he'd entered the canteen, he couldn't hold it back. "You!" he said as he pointed at the man and stormed over to him.

The low level of conversation died down as Flynn weaved

through the tables towards the bearded man. Contempt stared back at him when he got close.

About ten metres between them and Flynn pointed at Brian again. "I hope you're proud."

"What are you talking about?" Brian said with a laugh beneath his words and a sneer on his fat face.

"Like you don't know. You and your gang of cowards are the reason she's gone."

Brian simply stared at Flynn.

Fire rose beneath Flynn's cheeks and he shook as he glared at the man. Sweat bled into the crushed ball of paper in his hand and his breathing sped up.

The silence swelled through the place until Brian finally said, "You're not making much sense, *boy*."

Tension snapped Flynn's shoulders tight and dragged them up to his neck. "Don't call me *boy*, you fat fuck. She's gone. You know full well she's gone."

Raised eyebrows and another laugh before Brian looked at Sharon and Dan. He then returned his attention to Flynn. "*Who's* gone?"

When Flynn shouted, the sound of it echoed through the large space. "Vicky, you moron!" He stepped closer so just a few metres separated them and clenched his fists so hard his forearms ached. "Vicky's *gone*! Driven away by you and your band of cowards."

"*We* didn't drive her away," Sharon said.

But Flynn ignored her and continued to address Brian. "She did more for you than you'll ever know, and you drove her out of here."

Again, Brian said nothing.

"I have no one now because of you."

At that moment Dan stood up. "*We* don't have any children!"

"That was Moira, not Vicky, you *idiot*."

"You need to learn some respect, boy." Dan moved closer to Flynn.

Flynn stepped forward to meet him. He might have only been sixteen, but he stood a couple of inches taller than Dan and had far more battle experience.

Just an inch separated their noses when Flynn said, "And you want to be the one to teach it to me, do you?"

The silence seemed to suck the air from the room and Flynn felt everyone in the canteen watching them. He shifted another half an inch closer and felt Dan's body heat against his face. He spoke in a low growl. "Well?"

When someone grabbed Flynn from behind and spun him around, he raised his fist. The fight left him. "Serj?"

Sadness sat in Serj's deep brown eyes, his eyebrows raised in a pinch in the middle. "Come with me," he said and tugged on Flynn's arm again. He pulled him away from Dan.

"Sit down, Dan," Serj said.

At first, Dan didn't move. He simply stared at Serj, seemingly braver now the conflict looked less likely to happen.

"Please?" the Indian man urged with a weary sigh. "We've had enough fighting to last us a lifetime."

Dan pointed at Flynn. "Tell *him* that."

Serj didn't respond. Instead, he stared at Dan and Dan stared back before returning to his seat. He eyeballed Flynn as he sat down.

Flynn couldn't keep it in. "Oh, sure"—his loud voice carried through the canteen—"he's brave now he's been asked to sit down. Now Serj has diffused the situation, you've suddenly discovered your spine."

"Shut up, Flynn!" Serj said.

Fire rushed up in Flynn, but he swallowed it back down again. Of all the people left in Home, he trusted just one of them. A deep inhale and he kept his mouth shut.

The sound of Flynn's and Serj's footsteps called through the canteen as Flynn followed the leader of Home to the foyer. The collective attention of the room burned into him still, but fuck them. Fuck them all.

***

When they reached the foyer, Flynn watched Serj walk over to the windows and look out. For a few seconds he stared at the diseased as if looking for faces he recognised.

Flynn stayed put. The diseased were creatures and nothing more. He didn't need to see familiarity in their twisted expressions.

When he'd finished, Serj turned to Flynn and spoke in a quiet voice. "She *chose* to go, mate."

The sounds in the canteen had picked up a little, the white noise of collective chatter showing Flynn they weren't listening to him and Serj anymore. Still, he kept his voice low. "Hardly a choice though, was it?"

"What do you mean?"

"Well, those lot in there didn't exactly give her many options. And why didn't *you* try to stop her?"

At that moment, Serj looked at the floor and let go of a weary sigh. "I would have stopped it if I could have."

"*It?*"

"*Her.*" A shake of his head as if to clear his mind and Serj said, "Her. I would have stopped her if I could have. It had to happen."

Flynn's rage resurfaced. "What the fuck are you talking about? The war *had* to happen. Vicky choosing to leave didn't have to happen. That definitely didn't have to happen."

When Serj stepped forward, Flynn tensed up and scowled at him.

"I'm sorry," Serj said as he got closer. "I'm sorry about everything. I want you to know I'm here for you whenever you need me. I promised Vicky I'd look out for you."

Another look into the sad deep brown eyes of Home's leader and Flynn's rage left him. His bottom lip bent out of shape and the lump he'd been pushing down rose up, wedging in his throat like a dry ball of bread. Although he drew a deep breath, the foyer around him still blurred through his tears. His bottom lip bent out of shape. He tried to say the word, but only managed to mouth it. *Why?*

Serj stepped forward and hugged him.

The man's embrace broke Flynn and everything rushed out of him. Hot tears burned his eyes and soaked his cheeks. He'd lost his mum and dad, and now Vicky. Sobbing, he shook his head into Serj's shoulder as he finally got his words out. "Why, Serj? Why?"

But Serj didn't respond. Instead, Flynn felt him grip tighter as he too shook with his own grief.

Chapter One

TEN YEARS LATER

They hadn't moved any quicker than a fast walk, yet the hot June sun burned strong enough to lift sweat on Flynn's body. He had to squint against the glare as he stared into the distance at their destination, a tight grip on his baton.

The town on the horizon stood as a skeleton of what it used to be, picked clean of anything useful. Only desperation and hope kept them coming back. Maybe it would have the supplies they needed. Maybe they hadn't checked every inch of it already.

A look at Serj, and Flynn saw him also squinting against the glare of the summer day. "Do you think we'll find the lead in there?"

Serj shrugged. "Dunno. It gets us out for the day at least, eh? Good to stretch our legs."

"That depends," Flynn said.

"On what?"

"On what we meet in the city. The more years that pass, the

more feral the human race seems to be getting."

Although Serj opened his mouth to respond, the words remained in his gaping jaw as he looked behind them.

When Flynn heard the voices too, he also looked over his shoulder.

They didn't need to have a discussion about it, they'd dealt with threats a thousand times before. As one, they dropped down into the long grass.

The people were still far enough away for Flynn to duck walk over to one of the rusty trucks on the old road without being noticed. The ground felt uneven beneath his feet. What used to be a highway now existed as broken lumps of concrete and asphalt. Nature had won, the grass slowly growing through it and tearing it apart over the years.

Where he'd sweated a little before, Flynn now had to wipe his brow with his sleeve to stop it running into his eyes. He leaned against the body of the old truck and kept a tight grip on his baton. If he pressed against the rusty vehicle too hard, it felt like the thing would turn to dust.

The grass stood at least a metre tall. That seemed to be about the optimum height for it in this area. For years it had remained the same. It made Serj completely invisible from Flynn's current position. Until the gang passed, they were on their own.

The loud voices of men and women drew closer. The abandoned cars marked out the old road, and despite it not being there anymore, Flynn and Serj always walked down it. A force of habit the gang had also seemed to adopt.

Flynn fought against his panic and drew long and slow breaths. Although his rapid heart begged for him to breathe quicker, his head, close to spinning out, fought against his natural reaction to fear.

As each breath satisfied him less than the previous one, Flynn gave in and breathed faster. Of course he wouldn't be able to calm himself down. There might be no diseased left in their part of the world, but the humans who remained were worse in a lot of cases. Especially marauding gangs like this lot; at least the diseased were predictable.

A glance up through the long grass and Flynn saw the head of one of the men. He wore what looked like the top half of a human skull as a cap. Dirt streaked his hairy face, gathering in his weathered wrinkles and drawing black lines on his skin. His wild eyes sat wide as he scanned the area. Tension coiled in his body, lifting his shoulders while he clenched his jaw. He looked on the very edge of losing his shit.

When the man pulled something up to his mouth and took a bite, Flynn's stomach flipped. A human arm, it had been cooked, the outside slightly charred, the split skin revealing lightning streaks of pink flesh beneath. More animal than human, the man chewed as he walked.

The man disappeared from view for a few seconds while he passed on the other side of the rusty truck. The grass swooshed in his wake as he ploughed through it, and the sounds of all of the others' feet dragged over the lumpy ground.

Flynn held his breath as he shifted along the truck and he peered around to see the man on the other side. He wore a leather vest and had a belt with an old bloodstained machete hanging down from it.

When Flynn looked next to the machete, his stomach

lurched. As long as the blade next to it, it hung down, the stump end of it glistening from where it had been hacked off at the elbow. It had turned blue from where it hadn't been cooked yet. The lower part of an arm, it probably belonged to the same person as the one the man currently chowed down on.

Flynn pulled back out of sight and continued to lean lightly against the truck, his heavy pulse rocking through him. As he listened to the people pass, they said things to one another he couldn't make out. Toothless mouths and a strong accent made for a garbled and indecipherable slur.

***

It seemed to last an age, but the gang of people thinned out as they all passed. At a guess, Flynn would have put their number at maybe thirty. Over the years, he'd learned the best way to deal with nomads: get the fuck out of their way and let them through. Because they rarely stopped during the day, if you could avoid being seen for the time they were there, it would be safe to come out again.

What must have been one of the last people in the group suddenly called forward to the others. "Hawk!" she shouted.

Flynn gasped and raised his baton. The woman stood on the other side of the rusty truck.

A grunt came back at her.

"Deer!" she called out.

Not that Flynn could see them, but because the group had stopped, the silence allowed him to hear the animals running through the meadow next to the old road. His pulse spiked. The woman would have to pass him to get to them. He lifted his baton a little bit higher.

No one in the group spoke, but as one they rushed off the road toward the sounds. The woman on the other side of the truck moved slightly slower.

Flynn clenched his jaw as he listened to her pass through the long grass and he got ready to swing for her. At least he'd take one down before they had to either fight or run from the rest of them, and one less cannibal in a world chock-full of the fuckers wouldn't be a bad thing.

The swoosh of the woman's movement stopped. Before Flynn could look up, he heard one of the men call from the meadow beyond. "Swan, what is it?"

When Flynn looked up to his right, he saw the wild, almost animal face of the woman staring down at him.

She had her head tilted to one side as if she listened to him rather than looked at him. Blonde hair clogged with dirt, filthy skin, and very few teeth left in her mouth.

Flynn stared back at the bright and wide blue eyes of the woman.

"Swan!" The call came again.

She looked in the direction of the man's voice.

"What is it?"

At least that was what Flynn thought he'd said. Hard to tell.

She looked back at Flynn, her eyes narrowing as she snapped her head to the other side.

Chapter Two

Flynn and Swan continued to stare at one another. If she moved for him, he'd crack her skull. She might have animal reflexes from years of living like one, but he'd move quicker if he needed to.

The smell of the long grass ran up Flynn's nostrils when he pulled in a deep breath. He definitely had the beating of one of them, but an entire pack would overwhelm him and Serj.

In the few years since the nomadic groups had sprung up, they'd earned quite a reputation. Two men from Home, Mark and Alan, had a run-in with them a few years back and never returned. Others from their community found two skeletons picked clean of flesh a few days later. They had scrape marks on the inside of their skulls from where someone had eaten their brains. The nomads moved through the world like a plague, consuming anyone they could get their hands on.

"Swan?" The call came again, the wind tossing the grass around Flynn and the tattered lady.

Despite her twitching movements—her snapping of her head from one side to the other, her slightly pulled-back arms—

something in Swan still clung onto her humanity. Flynn saw it in the pinch of her blue eyes. Sadness stared out of them. Trauma from a hard life of atrocities. What had happened to her to land her with a bunch of savages? She stared regret down at Flynn. Empathy.

Flynn tensed in anticipation of yet another call from one of the gang before Swan snapped her head in the direction of the sound. "It's fine," she called back at them as an animalistic caw. "Thought I saw something. Nothing. Not a critter like I'd hoped. Nothing."

She turned her back on Flynn as if he didn't exist and headed in the direction of the others, picking her way through the long grass with stabbing steps.

Flynn let go of a breath that went on forever. As the air left his tense body, he turned limp, pressing into the rusty shell of the huge truck behind him.

Despite relaxing a little, Flynn still kept a tight grip on his baton. The nomads weren't known for their generosity; to take her at her word would be foolish.

Chapter Three

About ten minutes passed before Flynn saw Serj appear.

After he'd looked down at Flynn, Serj turned and looked behind him in the direction the nomads had gone. "I think we're okay now."

Flynn stood up and was momentarily dazzled by the sun. He too scanned the meadow, the grass moving with the wind. "I think I preferred it when the diseased were here. At least we knew what they'd do."

"And what's with all the animal names?" Serj said.

"I've got a theory about that."

"Go on."

"If they give themselves animal names," Flynn said, "behave more animalistic, and communicate in a series of short sentences and grunts, then they're regressing from humanity, right?"

Serj shrugged. "Okay."

"Well, it must be quite a thing to get your head around. Eating people, I mean. Anything to make it slightly easier …"

"Like pretending you're not human, distancing yourself from the atrocity of it?"

"Exactly."

Another shrug and Serj looked at the town on the horizon, the sun high in the sky above it. "This place always reminds me of her, you know."

Flynn would be lying if he said he didn't see it coming. He and Serj had been into town several times in the past few years and Vicky always came up. Instead of looking at Home's leader, he looked at the broken office block that dominated the craggy skyline. What had once been a town now looked like jagged shards pointing at the sky.

"I can't believe it's been ten years," Serj said.

Tension pulled Flynn's back tight. Did Serj really need to go there with this?

"And I can't believe it's been eight years since the last of the diseased died off."

"You think they're all gone?" Flynn asked.

"I don't know. I hope so."

"I keep thinking she'll come back," Flynn said, the words falling from his mouth before he could stop them. "I know it's been years, and logic would tell me I'm a fool to have any kind of hope, but I'd give *anything* to see her again. To ask her why she left."

Serj continued to stare at the town in front of them. "What do you think she'd make of things now?"

"Of Brian and his lot running Home?"

"*Hey!*" Serj turned to Flynn. "They *don't* run Home."

"As good as. Were it not for you, they'd take the place over in a heartbeat."

"That's why I stop them!" Serj said.

The sound of the wind carried over the vast meadow.

Flynn finally spoke. "Do you think she'll *ever* come back?"

"I don't know, mate."

The tension that had coiled in Flynn's back moved to his jaw and he bit down hard. His pulse quickened. He still had a hold of his baton and he squeezed it tighter than ever. "Why did she leave? Did I do something wrong? Was I too moody with her?"

"No!"

Flynn shook his head and heat rose up beneath his cheeks. "How do you know? No matter how many times I run through what happened in my head, I just can't understand it. I was *sixteen*, for fuck's sake."

Flynn watched several birds flying over the ruined town in the distance. "All she wanted was to mother me, yet she left. What was wrong with her? I was a fucking child. I needed her and she didn't give a fuck. She didn't give a fuck about anyone but herself."

Another few seconds passed where neither of them spoke. Serj broke the silence this time. "It's like a hot coal, you know?"

"What is?"

"No matter who you throw it at, you'll still get burned."

"What are you talking about?"

"Anger, Flynn."

"You think I don't have a right to be angry?"

"I didn't say that. But you've held it for a long time."

Fire rushed through Flynn and he raised his voice. "That's because she left me!"

"Maybe it was more complicated than that."

Before Flynn could reply, Serj added, "And even if it wasn't, you need to find a way to stop it burning you."

"And how do I do that?"

"Forgive her. Whatever reasons she had, we both know how much she loved you. She made a choice. Whether it was a good or a bad one, she loved you nonetheless. And if you can't do it for her, do it for yourself. You need to find a way to let go of your hurt because it'll consume you. It'll mess with every relationship you have and keep on stinging you until you overcome it."

Flynn refused to look at Serj, the wind stinging his already sore eyes. He ground his jaw and breathed through his nose.

When Serj nudged Flynn, he squeezed his baton harder.

Serj said, "What do you think she'd say if she could meet Angelica?"

"She knew Angelica," Flynn said.

"Not when she was your girlfriend."

Heat spread through Flynn's cheeks and he didn't reply.

"Come on," Serj said, "you've been together for two years now. It's okay to call her your girlfriend. I reckon she'd cry with happiness. You were her baby boy."

A couple of heavy gulps and Flynn shook his head. When he looked at Serj, he saw the man's intention and relaxed a little. Another gulp against the burning lump in his throat and he nodded. "I think she'd cry too."

A broad smile spread across Serj's face.

"Thank you," Flynn said.

"For what?"

"I needed someone when Piotr died and Vicky went away. You didn't have to do it, but you were there for me and I'll never forget that."

"Does that mean I have to cry about you and Angelica now?" Flynn couldn't suppress his smile when he looked at Serj.

"Come on," Serj said and nudged Flynn again. "Let's go and see if we can find some lead in that cursed town."

Chapter Four

"So, what about you?" Flynn said to Serj with a smile, his voice echoing as they passed beneath the railway bridge leading into the town.

"Huh?" Serj said, his attention fixed firmly in front of them as they walked.

"Come on, you old dog, don't hold out on me. I've seen the way Sally looks at you. You can't tell me there's nothing there."

Unlike a lot of the town, the railway bridge remained standing. It probably wouldn't hold up against a train going over it anymore, and bricks had fallen from it to the ground, but it hadn't collapsed yet. Their footsteps were amplified from walking beneath it. Flynn looked at the structure above their heads. Hopefully it wouldn't fall at that moment.

Once they'd stepped out of the other side, Serj looked up at the vast abandoned office building in front of them. "I'm not interested," he said.

Flynn looked away from his friend and up at the structure too. What had once been a modern building made from steel and glass now stood as a skeleton of its former self. Much of the metal had been stripped from it—and anything else useful by the look of things.

The old office furniture remained on the sparse floors. Many of the cheap desks had buckled and folded down on themselves where years of damp had eaten away at their weak chipboard. The chairs lay scattered around, their covers ripped, exposing the foam inside them.

"After Jessica," Serj continued, "I kind of lost interest in women, you know?"

A nod of his head and Flynn said, "That's understandable." Serj clearly didn't want to talk about it, so he looked at the spray-painted words on the walls of the place. If they could even be called that. He couldn't make out most of the writing, but he did see one phrase repeated over and over. *KEEP OUT!*

"People have been picking this town clean for twenty years now," Flynn said. "You think there'll be anything left for us? Especially with how useful lead is?"

"I hope so. We only need a small bit, so I'm sure we can find it. Just enough to line the barn's chimney. We're losing about ten percent of our supplies to that bloody leak, or about ten percent of storage space. We need to sort it out, especially before winter."

Although Flynn listened to Serj, he couldn't help but look at the red paint. The aggressive warning that told them to get the fuck away. "And you think the rats will let us in and out again without any problem?"

A shrug of his shoulders and Serj said, "Who knows? They may write all that on the walls, but they've always seemed to avoid conflict before. This is the closest place to find any buildings, so we've got to try, right?"

Another look at the red writing and Flynn didn't reply.

While craning his neck as if he could see around the large building in front of them, Serj said, "There's got to be a small amount of lead left on one of the roofs. Come on, we can be in and out in no time."

Serj took off at a jog around the left side of the large building and Flynn followed him, still clinging onto his baton. Not that it would do him any good. If the rats turned on them, they'd be fucked, outnumbered potentially in the hundreds.

The pair moved at a steady jog. They could find more speed if they needed it.

As they ran, Flynn looked into the old, abandoned shops. Impossible to tell what many of them had been, the signs had all fallen down and the insides picked clean of anything useful. It seemed wherever he looked he saw the rats' indecipherable scrawl. He could only make out the two repeated words: *KEEP OUT!*

The wind played its symphony through the abandoned buildings, dragging Flynn's attention to his left and right. He knew the noise to be the wind, but he still had to check, just in case.

Most of the buildings had collapsed in on themselves. Maybe from the effects of neglect, but more than likely human intervention. If you took enough from a building, it would inevitably fall. No wonder the rats were so pissed off about it.

As they jogged into what used to be a pedestrian area in the high street, Flynn caught movement in the shadows to his right. It shifted through the darkness and vanished before he'd seen it clearly. Another scuffle on his left and Flynn saw something, but not enough to get a clear picture of what. He and Serj shared a look with one another.

"Rats," Serj said in a low voice. "They'll leave us be if we leave them be."

"I'm glad you're confident," Flynn said as he watched the shops for more of them.

Every shop Flynn looked into had the mark of the rats in it. The words *KEEP OUT* and red spray-painted lines of other words they'd tried to recreate. Maybe the rats understood what had been written. Maybe their language had evolved rather than devolved. Although hard to believe when he looked at the infantile scrawl.

Out of breath from the run, Flynn said, "Pretty fucking clear they don't want us here."

Although Serj frowned and looked into the shops—his heavy steps slapping down on the concrete ground—he didn't reply. When he looked forward again, he pointed in the direction they were heading and said, "There."

Flynn looked, but he couldn't see what Serj had seen.

"The fire exit stairs," Serj said. "That'll give us access to the roof up there. It looks relatively untouched."

Flynn looked at the large wall with the metal stairs zigzagging up the side of it. The roof on the top hadn't folded in like most of the others had. "Those stairs don't look very solid."

Serj didn't reply. Instead, he picked up his pace and headed for the wall.

Chapter Five

The *tock* of Serj's feet called out through the near silent town as he climbed the metal stairs.

Flynn climbed up after him, checking behind frequently for signs of the rats. He and Serj were exposing themselves and leaving just one way down. Time to find out if the little fuckers were hostile or not.

The stairs rocked as they climbed them, but when Flynn looked at the points where they'd been anchored to the walls, they seemed stable. Although *seemed* could quite easily be proven wrong.

The scuff of more feet moved over the shop's dusty floors below. Flynn looked back again. Shadows spilled out into the high street and betrayed the movement of the hidden rats, but he couldn't see any of them yet. It served as a potent warning; they were in their space now and they operated only with their permission.

When they reached the top of the stairs, they were five storeys up. Flynn turned around and looked out over the town. The unobstructed wind crashed into him and cooled his sweat-dampened skin.

"There's some," Serj said as he pointed over the roof, his hair being tousled by the strong breeze. He didn't seem concerned with keeping his voice down.

Flynn looked down to see agitation twitch through the shadows below before he looked to where Serj pointed. Lead stretched up the side of the large chimney.

"That chimney's bigger than ours, right?" Serj said.

Flynn nodded before he looked back down at the ground. The shadows had grown larger from where the rats had moved to the very edges of the buildings. Just out of sight, they seemed ready to reveal themselves.

"If we can get that lead free, that should be enough." Serj stepped onto the roof.

A loud *snap* popped through the town and, before Flynn knew what had happened, Serj vanished from his sight.

Chapter Six

The shadows in the doorways pulled back as Flynn ran down the fire escape. Maybe they didn't mean him any harm, but if they tried anything now, he'd kill the fucking lot of them.

The sound of Flynn's feet hammered down the stairs, the entire staircase rocking with his movement. "Hang on, Serj," he called out. Fuck knew if he heard him or not.

When he got to the last flight of stairs, Flynn vaulted over the handrail and hit the ground running. He ran alongside the wall and around to the front of the shop Serj had fallen into.

Like with every shop, a huge empty space sat where the window used to be. It left a large gap for him to run through.

The second he saw Serj, Flynn pulled up and clapped a hand to his mouth. "Oh God."

Where Flynn would have expected anyone to scream in Serj's situation, he found his old friend didn't. Instead, he simply lay on the ground, a pool of blood spreading around him as he held the long metal bar that had pierced up through his stomach.

A scaffolding pipe or something similar, Serj had landed on it back first. The old pole shone with blood as it pointed at the sky, an accusation to the gods for letting this happen.

When Flynn grabbed Serj, his Indian friend winced and he shook his head. "Don't," he said, the word a wheeze more than anything.

"What then?" Flynn asked as he turned his face away from the stench of Serj's torn bowels.

The deep mahogany gaze that had always been there for Flynn seemed to fade as Serj looked at him. Instead of speaking, the man simply shook his head.

"No," Flynn cried, his voice calling out through the quiet town. "There must be something we can do."

Again, Serj simply shook his head as he fought for breath.

For a few seconds, Serj flapped his right arm in the direction of his hip. Clumsy with his rapidly draining essence, it took him a few attempts to clamp a hand on his knife. He shook as he worked it free and handed it to Flynn.

"What's this for?" Flynn asked, the knife's handle sticky with Serj's blood.

"I need you to end it for me."

"What?!" Flynn's voice startled a bird nearby, which took off and flew out through the open shopfront.

"It's no good," Serj said. "I can't get off this pole and I don't want to try. This is the end for me."

"No," Flynn said and dropped the knife. He held Serj's right hand with both of his.

The same serene stare Flynn knew so well fixed on him. "Please do this for me. I won't make it back to Home. Look at me …" He stopped and winced, catching his breath before he added, "I'm bleeding out as it is. You pull me off this pole and I'll split."

"Then I'll go and get someone from Home to come and help."

"You think I'll last that long? Besides, what do you think will happen when you leave me here?"

When Serj looked up, Flynn did the same. There must have been at least fifteen to twenty kids hanging around. They were on the first floor of the shop, looking down through the huge hole Serj had made when he fell.

Dirty faces, long hair, tatty clothes, and wild eyes. The rats ranged in ages from about six to twelve. If the rumours were accurate, Flynn could only see a handful of them. Apparently hundreds of them lived in the town—although rumours had a way of stretching the truth.

It had been said that the kids moved in when their community fell to a vicious group of nomads. Every adult and teenager had been slaughtered, but the young children had been set free. Since then, a lot of local groups had fed them, but it would seem no one wanted the responsibility of taking them in. Serj had even sent people from Home to deliver them food. They left care packages in the centre of town, which the kids picked up after they'd gone.

Some people believed they had adults with them and the kids were just a front to get charity. Flynn saw the logic in it; people did what they could to survive. The red paint on the walls was probably an attempt to fake childish illiteracy.

Regardless of what he believed, Flynn shuddered to look at them. They were feral and gaunt. Desperate for sustenance in whichever way they could take it. They didn't look ready to attack, but if Flynn left a wounded Serj, they'd gladly take the care package.

Even as Flynn said the words, he understood just how empty they were. He had no hope against the army of kids. "They won't fucking touch you. I'll take them all down if I have to."

Fifteen to twenty pairs of eyes stared down at him. Who was he kidding?

A look back at Serj and Flynn couldn't see any other options than the one presented to him. Yet he still said, "I'm not killing you"—his voice shaking and his eyes stinging with the start of his tears—"I *can't.*"

Serj closed his eyes as he nodded. "You *need* to. You can't leave me like this."

At that moment, Flynn got to his feet and shouted, "Fuck!" He kicked an empty plastic bottle, which skittered across the floor and clattered into one of the walls. Even louder than his previous shout, Flynn's call echoed through the empty space when he screamed, "Fuck!"

***

After he'd paced for a minute or so, Flynn hunched down next to Serj and picked his hand up again, but left his knife on the ground. Tears soaked his cheeks and he watched Serj close his eyes, his breaths coming more heavily than before. Every few seconds, a wince of pain twisted his friend's face.

When Serj opened his eyes again, it took him a few seconds to focus on Flynn. "Vicky would have done this for me."

"Fuck Vicky!" Flynn snapped back, his entire body pulling tight at the mention of her. "If she would have done it, I'm inclined to do the exact opposite. She lost my respect the second she walked out."

Several heavy breaths and Serj forced his words out. "She loved you more than anything, you know?"

"If she loved me more than anything, then why did she leave me?"

For the first time since Flynn had known him, Serj cried. His entire face twisted with fear and he shook where he lay. "Please, Flynn. Please do this for me."

The one person who hadn't let him down in his life. The one person who'd always been there for him and never asked for anything in return. The one person who'd been there when Flynn needed him most. He drew a deep breath and lifted the knife. A glance up at the rats and he saw more had gathered around the hole.

He turned away from the kids. They'd seen he had no choice; he had to do what his friend asked of him. A weak grip on Serj's knife and Flynn raised it up. He looked down at his crying friend and he shook his head. "I'm so sorry, Serj. I love you, man."

Just as Flynn clenched his jaw and squeezed a tighter grip on the knife, Serj said, "Stop!"

Flynn paused.

After several heavy breaths, Serj forced his words out. "I need to tell you something about Vicky."

Chapter Seven

As much as Flynn wanted to be patient, Serj didn't have long left. His frame locked tight as he watched Serj gasp and splutter on the dusty ground. "What is it?" he said. "What do you need to tell me about Vicky?"

It took a few more breaths before Serj found enough force to drive his words out. He shook his head as he said it, the shine in his eyes dimming. "She didn't leave you."

The dirty, abandoned shop around Flynn seemed to shift as if his perspective of it went off-kilter. Hell, the entire fucking world jolted on its axis. "What do you mean?"

Another shake of his head and Serj pulled several more breaths into his body. The smell of blood hung in the air. A rush of wind flew into the shop and Flynn caught movement in his peripheral vision—just a loose piece of paper flapping in the breeze.

More rats gathered around the hole and peered down. Their already wide eyes had widened further. Their hunger seemed to be pulling them forwards as they all leaned over the hole and stared at the dying Serj. Apparently they preferred their meat alive. Although, like many stories about the rats, the rumours probably weren't true. The adults, wherever they were, would probably cook the flesh once the kids brought it back to them.

"She was forced out," Serj finally said.

"Forced out?!" Flynn noticed the rats flinch in response to his outburst. "Forced out by *who*?"

A lethargic turn of his head and Serj stared straight at Flynn. He didn't need to say it.

"Brian, Sharon, and Dan? Because of their kids?"

The pause only lasted a few seconds, but it felt like a lifetime. "No," Serj said. "They found out."

A chill ran from Flynn's head to his toes. "You mean about the virus? About her part in it?"

Before Serj could respond, something fell from the hole and Flynn ripped his knife up and pointed it in the direction of the small girl. No more than eight years old, she had scruffy brown hair and a ripped nightie covering her skinny form. The way she stood there, hunched over, suggested she'd jumped rather than fallen.

She stared at Flynn and then the knife before she pulled her lips back in a snarl, baring her yellow teeth.

Her hiss ran needles into the base of Flynn's neck and his shoulders lifted. When she snapped her hand out, he barely saw it move. However, he did see the bug in her pinch. A cockroach, it twisted and writhed before she put it into her mouth.

They shared a look while she chewed on the insect and then she sprinted from the room through a door at the back. Fuck knew where it led, but as long as she left them alone, he didn't care.

After he'd glanced up at the others to make sure no more would come down, Flynn looked back at Serj. "They found out she helped set the virus free?"

Serj nodded.

"Because *I* said it in Home?"

Serj nodded again, although even that seemed to be taking its toll on him now. His movements were weak, his sweating face pale.

Although Flynn drew a breath to speak, Serj cut him off. "She wanted you to think she'd left so you'd stay safe in Home. She loved you and wanted to make sure you'd be okay. Home was the best place for you and she didn't want anything to jeopardise that. She had to die regardless and saw no point in you having to leave also."

Already limp, Serj fell even more flaccid, every word taking its pound of flesh from him.

Flynn looked up at the rats again before he glanced down at his boots. It seemed impossible that a body could lose so much blood and not be dead. "But why are you telling me now?"

"You needed to know …"

"The truth?" Flynn finished for him and looked up again at the rats.

Serj nodded.

Now he'd got the words from his friend, Flynn shook more violently than before. A mixture of hurt and rage swirled within him. "I'll kill 'em," he said. He shook his head as he stared down at the glossy pool of blood on the ground, the shifting silhouettes of the rats reflected in it. "I'll kill all three of the fuckers. Suffocate them in their sleep. I'll make sure they pay."

"Remember what I said about the hot coal?" Serj said, sweat running from his brow down either temple.

"What the fuck are you talking about? They *killed* Vicky."

"But you killing them won't bring her back. I wanted you to know …" Serj's eyes closed for a second. When he opened them again, he said, "So you don't think ill of Vicky anymore. She did the best for you."

Flynn watched Serj turn so pale his skin looked to be on the way to translucent. When he saw it in his friend's eyes, Flynn said, "You think they were right to kick her out?"

"They had to."

"Because she set the virus loose?"

Serj dipped a feeble nod.

"Because the world's the way it is because of her?"

Another nod.

As much as Flynn wanted to argue, he couldn't. The world *had* become this way because of her. The crowd of rats above should be in school now and worrying about friendships and the latest craze. Instead, they lurked in the shadows, waiting for things to eat. God knew what other things happened to them when they were with the adults who clearly directed them. The haunted looks in their eyes spoke of something much darker than cannibalism. But maybe Flynn imagined it. More speculation about a group of people he knew nothing about.

A deep inhale lifted through Serj and he said, "Vicky said she would have done the same to someone else." His eyes rolled in his head and he sweated more than before. "Once the decision had been made, she just wanted to make sure you were okay."

The world turned blurry in front of Flynn, but it didn't stop his awareness of the ever-thickening press of bodies above. A glance, and even with his poor, tear-distorted vision, there looked to be double the amount again. They waited, but for how long?

"I just want to make sure you know how much she loved you. And that she *didn't* let you down." Serj nodded at the knife in Flynn's hand. "Please stop my pain now."

Flynn drew a deep breath, the metallic essence of Serj filling his senses again as he pulled the air in. He also smelled the dirt coming from the rats above him. If many more gathered up there, the ceiling would collapse beneath their weight.

Several blinks cleared Flynn's sight and he nodded at Serj, gripped the handle of his knife, and yelled out as he drove it into the top of his friend's head.

Physically, it felt no different than killing a diseased. The blade broke through the bone and sank into Serj's brain, turning him off.

When Flynn let go of his grip on the knife, it protruded from Serj's head. His dead eyes were spread wide.

It took all Flynn had to stand up. He stumbled back several paces before he looked up at the rats one last time. More still had gathered around the hole.

Clumsy with his steps, Flynn turned his back on the shop and shuffled through the space that had once held the front window.

By the time he'd stepped a few metres into the high street, he heard the rush of bodies swarming from the hole down towards Serj. At least they didn't get to take him alive.

Chapter Eight

Not physically exhausted, but emotionally fatigued, Flynn's legs trembled beneath his weight as he returned to Home. He'd walked over the new bridge crossing the river and currently moved through the long, grassy meadow outside their complex. The sun pushed down on the back of his head and the grass came up to his chest. On another day, it might have even been pleasant with the fresh meadow smell in the summer heat. But covered in the blood of his best friend and mentor and returning to a place full of enemies took away any appreciation he might have felt for the weather.

The wall around Home stood as strong and indomitable as ever. As the years went on, they'd chopped down trees, stripped them of their bark and branches, and stood them in a line like soldiers. Each one had been buried at least two metres into the ground and had been butted so closely to the one next to it, it would take a tank to knock them down. Since they'd built the wall, they might have had gangs pass the place, but no one had tried to attack. Many communities fortified themselves in this way now.

A sentry stood at either side of the gate, and when Flynn saw Brian as one of them, his stomach clenched tight as if jabbed with electricity. Bile lifted in his throat at the sight of the man, but he gulped down the bitter taste, clenched his jaw, and pushed forward.

The gates opened before Flynn got to them and he strode through into the complex. The usual smell of sewage hit him the second he entered the place and he screwed his nose up in response to it. Since the solar panels had gone, Home had fallen into complete disrepair. They used the underground complex to sleep in and not a lot else now. Some suggested moving the toilets outside the wall to get rid of the smell, but that would put them in too much danger every time they needed to make a trip to the john.

By the time Flynn had walked just a few metres into the place, Brian appeared at his side and said, "What happened?"

Serj's blood had dried against Flynn's skin, so when he closed both of his hands into fists, it cracked.

When Flynn didn't respond, Brian said, "Where's Serj?"

A clenched jaw and quickened pulse, Flynn looked at the barn with the leaking chimney. "We didn't get your lead."

"*Our* lead; it's for the good of the community."

Flynn looked across at the bearded man and growled. "We didn't get *your* lead."

Brian didn't argue again. "So what happened? I'm guessing that isn't your blood on your hands?"

"You'd know all about that, wouldn't you?"

Impatience twisted Brian's face and he focused a bitter scowl on Flynn. "What are you talking about?"

"Never mind," Flynn said and looked away from the man.

Many of Home's residents hadn't noticed Flynn's return yet. If he could keep it that way, it would save a lot of questions.

As Flynn passed through the place—as out of sight as possible—he watched the people working the farmland. Everyone who could work did. It made for a productive community. A community that would need to be saved from the tyrannical—or soon to be tyrannical—rule of Brian, Sharon, and Dan. Now Serj had gone, they had nothing stopping them. At least, they would think they had nothing stopping them.

Flynn focused his attention on Home's front door, hoping he'd remain invisible to the people in the community. It stood propped open as they always had it during the day. Now a dusty wreck of a place, they needed to ventilate Home as much as they could so when they locked it up at night it had at least been aired out.

"Flynn!"

A look to his right and Flynn saw some of the teenagers from Home.

Maggie had been the one to call to him and she led the group of six over to him at a jog. Genuine concern lit up her face when she saw the blood on him. "My god, what's happened? Is it Serj?"

As the heart of the community, everyone loved Serj—especially the young people. He'd been one of the only adults to listen to them. He treated them like human beings while the other guards treated them like dumb kids.

For a few seconds, Flynn bit down on his bottom lip to hold his grief back. He finally nodded. "Serj has gone." He looked over to see Brian had come close to listen in. "He fell when we were trying to get Brian's lead and he didn't make it."

Where Brian would usually respond, he didn't this time. He must have heard the thin ice cracking beneath his feet.

The group walked with Flynn as he headed towards Home's entrance. The door sat in the small hill, the once solar panel field behind it.

Where the solar panels had been, Flynn could now see a complex twisting of tubes and funnels raised in the air. From a distance, it looked like a huge marble run like the one they had for the children inside. It had been set up to catch and store water. Without the filtration system and the electric pumps, they'd had to adapt.

At the sight of Sharon and Dan, Flynn ground his jaw. They looked him up and down as they approached.

"What's happened?" Dan said.

Before Flynn could answer, he jumped to hear Brian speak behind him. "Serj is dead. He fell while collecting lead for the community."

"For *you*," Flynn said.

Again, Brian didn't argue with him. A shared look between Brian and Dan, and Dan didn't question it either.

"We're here for you, Flynn," Brian said as he reached over and touched Flynn's forearm.

Flynn stopped dead and glared at the bearded man. He reached down to the baton on his hip and lifted his lip in a snarl.

Brian removed his hand and lowered his eyes.

"Look," Sharon said, "I know you're upset about Serj, but that doesn't mean you should come back here and take it out on us."

A hard grip on his baton still and Flynn pulled in a deep breath. He could feel the attention of the teenagers on him. They didn't need to see this. Were it just him and the three guards, he'd cave in every one of their deceitful heads, but he couldn't do it here. Not now.

"Flynn!" Sharon said again as he walked away from her. "I *demand* you talk to me."

"I don't give a fuck what you demand, Sharon."

Sharon gasped, and although Flynn didn't look at them, he heard Brian say, "Leave it."

Flynn stopped again and turned around to face the three guards. "Just so you know, you don't get to demand anything of me ever again, okay? Serj has gone, so as far as I'm concerned, this place needs a new leader." He looked each of the three up and down. "Because from where I'm standing, we *don't* have a suitable replacement."

None of the guards challenged him, and when Flynn walked off again, they all remained where they were.

Chapter Nine

Flynn entered Home's foyer on his own and walked down the steps into the canteen. The blue linoleum floor had rips and scuffs all over it. Dents and holes from years of wear and tear, it needed replacing, but no one cared now with the outside a much safer place than it used to be.

The once white walls showed huge patches of exposed plaster beneath, and what paint remained had either blistered or looked ready to flake off.

The tables in the vast space were grubby and all shoved into one corner, and the wall of monitors sat as blank, dusty screens. One of them had fallen to the ground when the bracket had given out, and had a spider's web of cracks across the front of it.

The corridor towards Flynn's room had once smelled of bleach, but it now reeked of damp and dust. Daylight shone through the grates up above and a slight breeze ran down from them. With no power, they couldn't ventilate the place in any other way. It meant water ran into Home when it rained, and it froze in the winter, but at least they could breathe.

What little strength Flynn had left drained from him when

he reached his bedroom door. He grabbed the cold handle and his vision blurred. He'd held onto his grief until now.

When he entered his room, a candle had already been lit and he found Angelica waiting for him. Even through his teary view, Flynn saw her beauty. He fell forward and threw his arms around her. "Thank god you're here," he said, sobbing hard. "I needed to see you. Thank you." He pulled back and held her face with both of his hands, his lip buckling out of shape as he repeated, "Thank you."

Chapter Ten

Flynn woke up to find Angelica still asleep next to him. The single bed always made for a tight squeeze, but because they still stayed in separate rooms most of the time, it didn't matter to have a less comfortable night's sleep once in a while.

Flynn rolled over onto his back, leaned out of bed, and lit a candle close to them. No windows and no electricity meant the rooms were always dark when the doors were closed.

Exhausted from the previous day, Flynn remained on his back and stared up at the ceiling. Like the walls in the place, white flecks of paint had come off it and huge patches had fallen away to reveal the plaster beneath.

The bedding he used was the same duvet and sheet he'd had when he'd moved in with Vicky over a decade ago. Although he hand washed them, years of wear had left them covered in stains and threadbare. He could also feel the springs pushing up through his mattress. At some point he'd have to do like the others had and replace it with sacks stuffed with old rags.

A deep sigh to his right and Flynn turned to look at Angelica. She had green eyes, so vibrant they made him think of the pictures he'd seen in books of lush rainforests. "I love it when we wake up together," he said.

Angelica smiled but didn't respond.

"Thanks for staying last night, I needed the company."

Again, she smiled—clearly too soon for words at that moment.

Yesterday had been too raw for Flynn to talk about what happened with Serj, other than to tell Angelica he'd died. He couldn't tell her he'd killed him, or what he'd found out about Vicky. What Brian, Sharon, and Dan had done to her. Should he tell her at all? After all, they needed to live in Home still. To cause trouble could seriously backfire on both of them. She needed to know Serj had died, but maybe nothing else. Just as he drew a breath to speak, someone knocked on the door.

"Hello?" Flynn called out.

The door muffled the voice of what sounded like one of the younger children. "There's going to be a service outside in five minutes for Serj."

The kid didn't wait for a response, and Flynn listened to his footsteps run away up the corridor before he turned to Angelica. "A service? What the fuck?"

Flynn sat up in bed and grabbed his clothes from the day before. When he looked at Serj's blood on them, he threw them down and picked up some different trousers and a top, muttering to himself while he did it. "A fucking service! Who the fuck do they think they are?"

Although Angelica sat up in bed and watched him, Flynn couldn't look back at her. Too angry to talk, he stormed out of his room.

The grates shone bright spotlights down into the corridor as Flynn walked along it. Dust motes danced in the strong beams from where the kid had run away only moments earlier. Every time he passed beneath one, the summer heat warmed him for a second. Clearly late morning at least, he and Angelica had obviously overslept.

As Flynn marched through the dusty and dirty canteen, he couldn't see another soul. Filthy tables, broken screens, and the echoes of what had once been the hub of their community.

The second Flynn stepped out of Home's foyer, the sun blinded him and he had to blink against its glare. Not that his restricted vision prevented him from seeing the large crowd gathered there. It looked like all of Home had turned up.

As Flynn's sight recovered, he looked at the people and saw them all stare back at him. Some of his anger left him. He couldn't kick off now. Not in front of everyone.

Flynn laid eyes on Brian at the front of the group. Sharon stood on one side of him and Dan on the other. Brian nodded. "We wanted to make sure you were present for this," he said.

While grinding his jaw, Flynn stared at the three of them. They stood in front of the graves of their children and all the other people who'd died over the years.

"Okay," Brian said with a clap of his hands. "I think that's everyone. As you all know by now, we lost Serj yesterday to a tragic accident in the town."

Angelica emerged from Home's foyer and walked up next to Flynn. When she put a hand on the base of his back, he tensed at the contact.

"For as long as most of us can remember, Serj has been here.

One of the first few people to get let into the place, he's always been a valuable member of our community."

The empty bullshit made Flynn want to vomit and he continued to stare at the bearded man. When he got a chance, he'd cut his fucking throat.

"Serj was a rock in this community. I considered him one of my greatest friends."

It took all Flynn had to refrain from screaming in Brian's face at that moment. What the fuck? They fucking hated each other.

"When I asked people what they wanted to say about Serj," Brian said, "I got an overwhelming amount of responses, all with a similar tone." He used his fingers to count the points out. "He was kind, generous, always ready to listen and help. He had a lovely way about him. He was calm and a great mediator. He saw when people needed him and he offered himself freely and without condition."

The lump had never left Flynn's throat, but it swelled to see all the people in the crowd nodding their agreement. Packed together, they all seemed united in their grief for Serj.

He'd done it by consensus, but Brian had just described Serj perfectly. Another look at the crowd and Flynn saw all the people Serj had touched. The teenagers—who even in such a small society had distanced themselves from it as they managed their rampaging hormones—the cooks, the farm workers, the tailors. Every person there seemed to feel the loss of the great man.

As much as Flynn wanted to challenge Brian, he couldn't. As much as he wanted to go up to Sharon and Dan and bury a knife in their skulls, it would serve no purpose. Not now anyway.

Then Flynn looked at Janice, one of the farm workers. She hugged her little boy, Adam. The eight-year-old child cried into her stomach, and he saw what this community meant to them. It meant safety.

The teenagers—every one of them sobbing—wouldn't last outside Home for five minutes with the rats and nomads about. If Flynn destabilised the community by taking down the three leaders, Home could fall, and the innocent citizens would pay the price.

"Sharon, Dan, Flynn, and I will continue to run this place and will honour Serj's memory in every decision we make."

The thought of working with those three monsters curled as a tight lump in Flynn's gut, but the people all nodded in response to Brian's plans.

Home might not work for Flynn at that moment, but it worked for everyone else. He needed to respect that like Serj would have. Serj always thought of the greater good.

Flynn swallowed back the lump in his throat and looked at Angelica next to him. He might not have Serj and Vicky with him anymore, and the leaders of Home were complete arseholes, but at least he had her. Maybe he could make it work here. Maybe he could get his head down and accept the rule of the three vicious bastards up at the front of the group. Maybe some sacrifices were worth it.

Chapter Eleven

Pains ran across Flynn's back and he twisted his body to try to ease them. He'd been sat on his crappy bed for hours, staring at the floor with his head in his hands. He'd only gotten up when he needed to light another candle.

The naked flame flickered and threw shadows around the room. He watched the movement for the longest time through unfocused eyes. What else could he do? He had to lock himself away from everyone else. Like Vicky had told him on more than one occasion, if he didn't have anything nice to say …

The community worked. Hard for Flynn to accept with the crooks running the show, but it worked. It benefitted the majority and he couldn't be so selfish as to try to take that down because it didn't benefit him.

Besides, he had a good woman in Angelica. Someone he could make a life with. Also, Dan and Sharon had every right to be upset about their children, and Brian simply picked a side.

Flynn would have been pissed if he'd found out one of those fuckers played a part in releasing the virus on the world. They didn't love Vicky like he did, so why wouldn't they kick her out?

Even if Angelica didn't want to leave with him, they could start a family in Home. The walls made it safe and they farmed enough food to sustain them indefinitely.

Fuck knew how long had passed. Flynn sat up straight, rolled the aches from his shoulders again, and flipped his head from side to side, pushing his left ear to his left shoulder and then doing the same with the right. A twinge ran up each side of his back with the movement.

Finally finding the impetus to move, Flynn got to his feet. It had been hours since the funeral. He needed to go see Angelica.

***

When Flynn stepped out into the hallway, he got a better idea of the time of day from the natural spotlights shining down into the space. Not dark outside, but the fading light left a grey haze in the corridors. He'd spent most of the day inside. Many of Home's residents would be in their rooms by now, including Angelica.

As he walked along the dusty corridor to see his love, Flynn pulled his shoulders back and straightened his posture. He'd tell her everything, and if he cried, then so be it. She needed to know he'd killed Serj, and to understand why he found it hard to be around Brian, Dan, and Sharon. But he didn't blame them. Well, he wouldn't blame them with time, he just found it upsetting to be in their presence at the moment.

Would Angelica think him a coward if he told her he'd left his best friend's body to be feasted on by the rats? How would she be able to understand that decision without being there? He couldn't have carried him back, and to leave him for any length of time was to give him over to them anyway. A shiver snapped through him to think of the hungry, little faces and the way they'd peered down through the hole at him.

At least if Flynn explained himself, it would help her understand why he'd needed the day on his own. Why he'd walked off without an explanation.

When he arrived at Angelica's room, Flynn looked up and down the deserted corridor. In the short time it had taken him to get there, the natural spotlights had darkened a little more.

A look at her door and Flynn saw where the paint had blistered away a long time ago. Like many of the doors and walls in home, the white glossy coat had come off to expose the wood beneath. Angelica had purposefully picked it away in the shape of a heart.

Flynn smiled at it. At least he had her in his life still. He knocked, the loud rap running both ways up the corridor.

The soft voice of his love whispered from the other side, "Come in."

One final breath to settle the nervous butterflies and Flynn entered the room. It didn't matter if he cried in front of her. She'd seen it already, and he should be upset with everything that had happened.

To see her standing in the middle of her room—her candles casting an orange glow over her beauty—lit Flynn up. The sadness of the day had slightly duller edges already, and he smiled at her radiance. "Angelica—"

"Wait," she replied, cutting him off.

Flynn frowned at the turmoil he saw play out on her face. "Wait?"

"Before you say anything," she said, "I need to tell you something."

A chill ran from the top of Flynn's head down as if ice had just been dumped on him. He'd felt the same chill when he'd read the letter from Vicky. The same chill when he'd watched his dad get dragged into the river. The same chill when he'd had to kill Serj. When he'd listened to the rats rush down to eat his friend. The chill that told him his life would change at that moment. He shook his head at her and the grief of the past few days rushed forward, wobbling his words. "Don't say it, *please*."

A deep sigh and Angelica looked down at her feet while wringing her hands. "It's not you."

"Fucking hell! After two years you're going to use that bullshit line?"

When she looked up again, she glared a resolve at Flynn that forced him back a couple of paces. It showed him her mind had been made up. Whatever they'd had, they didn't have it anymore.

"Okay," she said and glared at him as she clearly let out her pain, "it *is* you. Mostly. I can see you have a lot of things inside you to work out. I can see how your parents dying, and then Vicky leaving, has fucked you up. And now, losing Serj on top of everything ... that's a lot to deal with. I can see how you have something wonderful inside you. Something great to give to the world, but you *never* give that to me. You *never* show me who you are. You *never* let yourself be vulnerable in front of me."

"What was last night, then?"

"That was the first time, Flynn." Her voice broke and her eyes glazed with tears. "You're *really* hard to love."

Although Flynn wanted to reply, he didn't.

"You're too distant. You're removed from everything around you. At first I thought you were cool—mysterious even—but after two years, you've barely let me past the surface. I need *more* from a relationship."

After he'd shot a puff of air through his pursed lips, Flynn said, "And to think I was coming here to open up to you."

"By spending the day locked in your room? Besides, this isn't about today, or now. This is about two *years* of neglect. Now is far too little far too late. I can't be in a relationship with you, Flynn. I need something more from the person I love."

Flynn opened his mouth to reply, but she cut him off. "I was waiting in your room when you got back from going out with Serj because I wanted to finish it with you then. But I couldn't, not with the state you were in."

The entire room spun and Flynn moved over to lean against a wall as he looked at his love. His heart kicked like it would burst through his chest and his body temperature rose. The lump in his throat solidified as a tumour from a lifetime of devastated relationships. And then he saw it. Something in her eyes. Sadness, sure, but he saw something else. Guilt … betrayal. Nausea turned over in his stomach. "It's Larry, isn't it?"

Instantly on the defensive, Angelica jabbed a finger at Flynn. "Don't you *dare* blame Larry for this."

She looked like she wanted to say more, but he'd heard enough. Flynn shook his head. "Fuck you," he said through clenched teeth. "Fuck you and Larry. I hope you're fucking miserable for the rest of your pathetic fucking lives."

Maybe he wanted a response. It would have been something

to see his words hurt her, but she didn't give it to him. Instead, she stared at him, the glaze of tears gone.

Flynn turned around and left her room. He slammed her door so hard it rang through the entire complex and kicked up a dust storm in the grimy corridor. Fuck her and Larry. Fuck everyone in Home. He didn't need them anymore.

Chapter Twelve

The vents in the hallway let the sound of night down into Home's corridors but did little to illuminate the empty walkway. Bugs and birds called down to Flynn as he walked with a lit candle from his room. He cupped his hand in front of it to prevent it from blowing out.

As he made his way down the corridor, Flynn rolled his shoulders to adjust the pack on his back. Yet to be filled, it still didn't fit as comfortably as he'd like. The straps had snapped so many times he had at least three knots tied into each one. Each knot found a different point around his shoulders and back to press into.

A metre or two around Flynn lit up from the candle's flickering flame. Beyond that, everywhere fell into darkness. It sounded clear, but for all he knew, someone could be watching him at that moment. They could see the large knife attached to his hip. Maybe understand the intention of his late night wanderings.

Although very few people walked the corridors at night, so he couldn't worry about it. But what if someone saw the light through the bottom of their door? A community full of people had to have a few insomniacs. Fuck it, he couldn't think about it.

When Flynn arrived at the room, he stopped and stared at the door. His heart sped up, pounding so hard he could almost hear it. Quicker breaths than before, his throat dried. Once he stepped into the room, there would be no going back.

A deep breath and Flynn pulled his long knife from his belt. He then unhooked the few lengths of rope that hung down from his backpack, rolled his shoulders one last time, and opened Brian's door as quietly as he could.

Chapter Thirteen

The fat fucker snored as he lay in his bed, oblivious to Flynn standing over him.

For a few seconds, Flynn simply stood there and watched the prick breathe. He could force the tip of his knife hard into Brian's eyeball and end everything there and then. He'd done it a thousand times with the diseased. Although, if he did that, he'd take away all the fun.

Instead, Flynn put his candle down on the side and properly took in the man's room. The paint fell from the walls like it did everywhere else, but most of the walls were covered by bookshelves. The bed lay in the middle, and a huge chair had been placed in each of the two corners farthest away from the door. They looked like thrones. Especially as they were a luxury very few others in the community had.

A shake of his head and Flynn got to work. As gently as he could, he unwound one of the lengths of rope and lay it over Brian's barrel chest. He dropped the rope down the other side of the man, hunched down and fished it back under the bed.

Once Flynn had looped the rope around the bed and had it

ready to tie, he repeated the process with another rope across Brian's middle. One would tie the top of his arms down and the other one the bottom. If he could disable his reach, he could overpower him.

When he had both ropes ready to pull tight, Flynn sat down on the floor next to the fat and bearded man, drew a deep breath, and pulled hard on the one running across his chest, pressing his feet against the bed frame to give him more tug.

It pinned Brian to the bed and woke him with a heavy gasp as it crushed the air from his lungs.

Although Brian's eyes flashed open, he didn't have time to react before Flynn tied a quick knot in the rope and tugged the next one to pin the bottom of his arms to the bed.

Awake enough to realise what had been done to him, Brian looked at Flynn. "You little fucker—"

He stopped short and his eyes spread wide when Flynn stood up and waved his knife at him.

"W-what are you going to do?"

Flynn said nothing. Instead, he used a third length of rope to tie Brian's legs to the bed. A glance at Brian and he could see the man looked like he wanted to fight, but another wave of his eight-inch knife quickly encouraged him to let go of his rage.

For the next two minutes or so, Flynn let the silence hang and paced up and down in Brian's room. He listened to the fat fuck breathe on the edge of a panic attack before he finally spoke. "So Serj told me what *actually* happened to Vicky. He said it wasn't fair for me to think she'd walked out when she'd been forced out."

Red-faced and breathing heavily, Brian spat as he spoke. "She couldn't stay here."

"That makes sense," Flynn said and let the silence hang again as he leaned over Brian and rested the sharp tip of his blade against the man's sweating cheek. "I can see how she *had* to leave."

"We had to give her the same treatment everybody else had when they were evicted. We couldn't risk her coming back."

"And *there* it is," Flynn said as he stood up straight again. "You *killed* her, Brian. I mean, you *had* to, right? And that's how you justify it to yourself. How you manage to sleep at night." He turned the knife so the flickering light bounced off its polished blade, and said, "Once you've had a fallout with someone, once you've gone past the point of no return, you have to follow through and kill them. There's no way back from that, eh?"

"She set the plague loose, Flynn. Besides, I wasn't the only one. Sharon and Dan wanted it too."

"Don't you worry about Sharon and Dan anymore."

"You've been to them already?"

"Two for the price of one, you fat fuck. Of course I went there first."

A single tear ran down Brian's red face and he shook his head. "Please, Flynn, please don't hurt me."

"Crocodile tears don't sit well with me, you know? You fucked her over, Brian, and you *have* to pay for that. That's how it works, isn't it?" Flynn rested the tip of his blade on Brian's cheek again, this time a little closer to his wide eye. "An eye for an eye and all that, right?"

"But—"

Flynn silenced the fat man with a raised hand. He then

rubbed his temples as if fending off a headache. "Your voice grates, Brian."

"But—"

"SHUT UP!"

Brian flinched away from Flynn's rage.

After a quick scan of his room, Flynn saw Brian's socks on the floor and he picked one of them up in a pinch. "My god, man, what the fuck's wrong with you? These socks are fucking disgusting!"

When Brian opened his mouth to respond, Flynn cut him off. "You don't need to answer that. I'm simply telling you you're disgusting. Worse than an animal. Worse than a diseased. And you know how easily I dispatched them, don't you?"

A look at the bookshelves and Flynn said, "A man is not great because of the books he owns. I wouldn't mind betting you've not read any of these."

Before Brian could say anything else, Flynn stuffed the sock in his fat mouth, jamming it in so hard the man heaved from either the taste of his own filth or from the fabric of the sock pressing against his gag reflex.

Another piece of rope, shorter than the others, and Flynn wrapped it around Brian's face, tying it so tight it cut into his fat jowls. "Your head's like a fucking pork joint. You *disgust* me."

Flynn spoke more to the knife than he did Brian at that moment, staring at the blade, mesmerised by the way the light danced along it. "Since before even Vicky left, I've dreamt of this moment. My chance to skin you. I've had practice with the wild animals we've caught, but I think it might be a bit messy still. I'm certainly no expert." A look at Brian and he grinned. "Hopefully it'll fucking hurt."

Although Brian screamed and writhed, the sock muffled most of his words. However, every time the fat fuck shifted on the bed, its metal frame groaned in protest.

Flynn looked down at the bed for a second before he said, "I'd shut up if I were you, fat man. Think of it like the fair. Scream if you want to go faster. That's what they used to say at the fair, right? I was six the last time I went, so I can't remember."

Brian watched Flynn through a confused frown and didn't answer.

"You're right." Flynn laughed. "I suppose it doesn't matter. Scream if you want more pain. How does that sound? It's not quite right, is it?"

Tears ran freely from the fat fuck's eyes and he trembled where he lay. Flynn clicked his fingers and laughed. "I've got it!" He pressed the tip of the knife into Brian's gut and said, "Scream if you want to go deeper. How's that?"

It looked like Brian had left the room; his disgusting body remained, but his eyes were glazed as if he'd retreated to a safer place.

"Serj said something else to me before he died, you know?"

Again, nothing from Brian.

"He told me anger's like a hot coal. And I've thought about that. I've thought long and hard. I think he's right; anger *is* like a hot coal. Throw it at someone and you get burned, right?"

Brian nodded furiously.

"But!" Flynn said and wagged his right index finger at Brian. "It's also a fuel. Coal, I mean. It fuels a lot of things. Like the desire to stick a fat fuck with a knife. With just one coal and a lot of patience, you can set fire to the world."

Flynn stuck the first centimetre of his blade into the top of Brian's right thigh. He watched the man shake his head and turn even redder. He watched his fat jaw bite down on his filthy sock. He watched him cry like a small child and he laughed harder than he'd laughed in years. A slow twist of the blade and he said, "That's it, Brian, scream if you want to go deeper."

Chapter Fourteen

Flynn hunched down in the darkness of Home's barn, his hands shaking with his urgency. He needed to get the pack loaded up and get the fuck out of there before anyone found out what he'd done. Unless he got unlucky, he should be good 'til morning, but by then he needed to be as far away from Home as possible.

Because he had to remain hidden, Flynn worked without light, pulling peppers, cucumbers, and tomatoes from their piles and stuffing them into his bag. In the short walk from Home to the barn, he'd seen the moon hung as no more than a fingernail in the sky. Sure it gave him the shadows to hide in, but it did little to help him see, even with the barn's door left wide open.

When he'd filled his backpack with as much as he could reasonably carry, Flynn shouldered his bag, picked his crossbow up, got to his feet, and left the barn.

Jackson and Ollie had pulled night duty on the gates that evening. As Flynn walked up to them, his heart beat out of control and his legs shook. They could ask to check his bag. Someone might find out what he'd done.

"Everything okay?" Jackson called out as he looked down on Flynn, a hand on his baseball bat.

"Yep," Flynn replied, the bag on his back seeming to treble in weight with the stolen goods. "I'm going out to do some night hunting. 'Bout time we had some meat in this place."

"Amen to that," Ollie said and he waved Flynn through. "Good luck, brother."

Even as he walked through the open gates, Flynn expected someone to call him back. But they didn't. How far would he get from the place before they realised what he'd done?

Chapter Fifteen

Flynn walked into the night, checking behind him every few metres. Far enough away that the boys on the gates wouldn't be able to see his paranoia, he could check back frequently to get a heads-up on a pursuing pack should they decide to give chase.

The heavy backpack pulled on Flynn as he walked, dragging the hard knots into his shoulders and sending a tingling sensation down both arms.

It hurt to hold his crossbow out in front of him, but with fuck-all vision ahead, he had to be ready for anything. When he'd lived with the diseased for so much of his life, he refused to trust things would be okay.

Flynn kept up a quick pace, sweat lifting on his brow and itching beneath his clothes. He forced a rhythm to his breaths to maintain the march and did his best to see through the dark and long grass.

By the time Home had been reduced to no more than a large silhouette on the horizon, Flynn released some of the tension in his body, but he still kept up his pace. He might lose sight of Home shortly, but he still needed to put as much distance between him and it as he possibly could. He'd never go back to that place again. Never.

***

The swoosh of the grass surrounded Flynn as he continued to plough through it. Hours had passed and he'd still not adjusted to the dark night. The human eye could only do so much.

Flynn looked around, for what good it did. The diseased didn't exist anymore, but it didn't matter how many times he told himself that. He only knew he hadn't seen any diseased in several years. That didn't mean he wouldn't see any again. Anyway, they had nomads and rats now. Although the rats kept to the town, so they'd be easy to avoid. Just the nomads, then. And maybe the diseased.

The hoot of an owl called out, and when Flynn turned in the direction of the sound, something moved through the undergrowth behind him. A fox or a badger? Maybe a diseased? No, it had to be an animal.

How had the boys on the gate believed he'd be going out to do some nocturnal hunting? Unless he had night-vision goggles on, he wouldn't be hunting shit. Any nocturnal creatures would be up and out of his way long before he even knew they were there.

Regardless of the ridiculously low odds, it was another reason for Flynn to keep his crossbow raised. He might get a chance to pinpoint a sound and take a lucky shot in the dark.

The ground grew more uneven as Flynn pushed on, the undulations beneath him twisting and turning his feet when he walked over them. He'd been nuts to leave at night. One hard twist and he could break his ankle. And what would he do then? A shake of his head and he pushed on. It didn't bear thinking about. Although, whether it bore thinking about or not, the thought of nomads chowing down on him like the diseased would have ran through his mind anyway.

A twig snapped behind Flynn and he spun around, his crossbow raised. The weak moonlight shone over the landscape and picked out a deer's silhouette for him.

Flynn's heart beat double time to look at the large creature. Far too much meat for one, but better to have too much than not enough. He'd do his best to make sure none of it went to waste.

The stock of the crossbow fitted neatly into Flynn's shoulder, so he rested it there and continued to take slow and deliberate steps forward. One eye closed, he looked down the barrel of his bow at his target.

Already pushing his luck, just ten metres separated Flynn and the creature before he stopped. He pulled in a deep breath and held it, his pulse booming through his skull. A gentle squeeze on the trigger and he bit on his bottom lip as he counted down in his head.

Three.

Two.

On *one* he let the bolt loose, the weapon kicking against his shoulder as the shot exploded away from him.

The bolt sank into the creature's body with a solid *thud*!

But the deer didn't move. It just stood there, motionless, like it had been the entire time. A tree would have flinched harder from being shot.

Just before Flynn could step any closer, what little he could see turned to darkness as a sack covered his head.

"Motherfuckers!" Flynn shouted before an explosion of white light hit his temple. The blow turned his legs weak and he fell to the ground.

Chapter Sixteen

Every time Flynn blinked, tendrils of pain ran from his eyeballs deep into his brain. A rock of nausea in his stomach and still dizzy from the blow he'd taken to the face, he sat up slowly. Very fucking slowly.

The dark room remained dark, showing it to be the reality of the place rather than a dimmed view through his foggy mind. Flaming torches ran down either wall. About a quarter of the size of the canteen in Home, the space looked like an underground cave. A dungeon.

The hard stone floor and walls were damp as if they sweated in the muggy heat of the place. It stank of dirt and body odour. Hard to tell exactly how many people he shared the space with. He could see ten at least, probably a few more.

"What the fuck?!" one of the people called out.

Although Flynn couldn't see well, he saw enough to make out the tall and stocky silhouette of a man as he stood up and hunched over another, skinnier man. "I said *what the fuck?*"

The skinny man on the ground didn't reply. Instead, he scrabbled backwards away from his aggressor, his frantic movements scraping through the place as everyone else watched on in silence.

"You'd best fucking answer me. What were you doing getting so close to me? What were you trying to achieve?"

The man on the ground shook his head and his voice came out as a high-pitched whine. "Nothing, I wasn't trying to do *anything*."

"Why were you getting close to me, then?" The deep boom of the aggressive man's voice shook through the place.

"I was just trying to see out of the cage. I'm number fifteen. It won't be long now."

"You won't even make it to then, you fuck." The fat man spat at the one on the ground. "I don't know who you think I am, but I don't believe your bullshit. You wanted to take me out before it starts, didn't you? You see me as a threat."

"No, it's not that, honestly."

"So you *don't* think I'm a threat?"

The man on the ground didn't reply. Probably for the best.

Movement by the cage door and Flynn saw several guards line up to watch events unfold. They looked like they could burst in at any moment and split the men up.

"I can't have anyone fucking with me. Especially not now, before we even get out there."

"I *promise*, I wasn't planning anything." By now, the cowering man had made it close to one wall and pushed himself up against it. The two women who'd been waiting there moved away and found somewhere else to sit.

Surely the guards had to come in at some point and put a stop to it.

Flynn flinched to watch the aggressive man kick the one on the ground. The deep slap of foot against flesh snapped through the place and the cowering man curled into a ball.

It should have been enough, but the large man kicked him again. "I know your game. I know what you had planned. I can't share this space with a scheming rat like you." He kicked him again and a lot of the people in the dungeon looked away. No one wanted any part of it.

A third kick, driven straight to the skinny man's kidneys, and the skinny man barked and wheezed while he fought for breath.

The large guy remained over the weak form of the other man and kicked him again and again. Each boot sent a deep *boom* through the dungeon. Each kick turned the weak man progressively weaker.

The guards still did nothing. One of them even leaned against the wall as if casually watching a sport play out in front of him.

When the aggressive man grabbed the other one's ankle and dragged him back into the middle of the room, Flynn moved to stand up. But a hand gripped his right forearm to stop him. He looked across at a blonde girl, who kept her hand on him and shook her head. She looked to be in her early twenties, and she looked like she understood the way of this place better than him. The bags beneath her eyes suggested she'd been there a while.

As Flynn looked into her wide stare, he felt her grip tighten on his arm. The pleading look on her face suggested she feared for his safety rather than her own.

Flynn let go of his desire to stand up, his face still throbbing from the blow he'd taken to it when they'd kidnapped him outside.

The first stamp cracked through the enclosed space. The

aggressive man wound up for a second one, lifted his foot above the weaker man, and stamped down on his face again.

Any fight the weak man had at that moment left him. Not that his aggressor stopped.

Another stamp on him and the weak man fell even more limp. Then another stamp, the heavy blow slipping off what must have been a face slick with blood. Another stamp, and another stamp, and another stamp.

One by one, the people in the prison all turned away until just Flynn watched the aggressive man. It might have been poorly lit, but the flaming torches showed him enough to see the tight grimace on the large man's face as he stamped the other guy's head to mush.

Maybe the other guy did have the intention of killing the larger man; maybe he didn't. Whatever the catalyst for the larger man's attack, it certainly sent a message: Don't fuck with him. He's the fucking daddy now.

When he'd finished, the dead man on the floor having turned limp quite some time ago, the large man panted, his shoulders hunched as he looked around the room. He stopped when he came to Flynn. "What the fuck are you looking at?"

Before Flynn could even think about standing up, the girl next to him grabbed him again. She stared at the ground as she spoke to him, clearly trying to avoid engaging with the aggressive man. "Don't, it's not worth it. Save your strength, you'll need it."

Although it felt hard to turn away from the open aggression in front of him, Flynn dropped his eyes and said nothing in response to the large man.

"Exactly," the man said. "And don't you lot forget what you've just witnessed. You fuck with me and I'll do this to you in a fucking heartbeat."

The large man seemed to have more to say, but just then, a female guard called into the cage, "He's awake! Number sixteen's awake."

At first, Flynn looked around the space to try to locate number sixteen. The girl next to him put a gentle hand on his back and said, "That's you, honey." Her soft touch wished him well.

Flynn tensed to watch five guards open the barred door at the front of the prison. Everyone in the cage—even the alpha male—moved out of the way.

As much as Flynn wanted to move too, he couldn't escape his fate. The guards were heading straight for him.

Three men and two women, they all carried long and rusty machetes. Hard to tell in the flickering light, but the weapons looked to be stained with blood. A slight glint ran along the edge of each one from where they'd been recently sharpened. Any shit from Flynn and they'd use them in a heartbeat.

As they got closer, Flynn backed away a little. "What the fuck's going on?" he said, looking first to the guards for answers and then at the blonde girl. "What's happening?"

But the guards didn't respond and neither did the girl. Instead, the one at the front kept his stride as he walked up to Flynn and kicked him square in the face.

A deep sting stretched away from Flynn's nose and he fell backwards. He tasted and smelled his own blood as it flooded his mouth, and for the second time that day, his world faded to black.

Chapter Seventeen

A different room to the dungeon, but equally as dingy, Flynn blinked against the darkness and breathed in the muggy, sweaty heat. The place smelled of mould, the humidity in the air stagnating in every crevice.

When Flynn tried to move, he met resistance almost immediately. Still groggy from being knocked out a second time, he tried to move again. His hands were trapped and level with his face. A look left and right, his movement restricted, and he saw he'd been put in a stock.

Before Flynn could speak, a woman appeared in front of him. Easily over six feet tall, she had wider shoulders than him and wore a long black apron. It looked to be made of leather, but he couldn't tell in the poor light. Much like the prison he'd only just been in, this one had torches on the walls and the flicker of them made the shadows shimmer.

After he'd looked around the room as much as the stock would allow, Flynn returned his attention to the woman. She smiled and said, "Welcome, number sixteen."

It might have been the first whack outside in the night that gave him the headache, it might have been the second in the dungeon, whichever one had been responsible for Flynn's pain, he now had to squint to ease it a little, even in the poor light. "Number sixteen?" he said. "What the fuck are you talking about?"

"Number fifteen came in before you and number seventeen will come in after."

"Well, that makes more sense, thanks for clearing it up."

"We already have number seventeen waiting," the woman said.

"No, we don't." The voice came from behind Flynn.

"Oh no." She smiled. "Thank you for reminding me. We don't have a number seventeen anymore. Our guards hit them a bit too hard. Or their skull was a bit too weak. I'm not sure which one." She looked back at Flynn. "You can call me Mistress, by the way."

"You can fuck off," Flynn said.

Mistress threw her head back and shoved her pelvis forward as she laughed. Genuine mirth—driven from her clearly large diaphragm—boomed through the small room. "Looks like we've caught a live one here."

The same voice that had spoken behind Flynn laughed with Mistress. Deeper than hers, it went off like an explosion. It sounded like a man. Like a monster of a man.

"Okay, sweetie," Mistress said as she put her hands on her knees and leaned close enough for Flynn to see half of her teeth at the back were missing. "Let's try to make this as painless as possible, yeah?"

"What the fuck are you on about?"

But Mistress didn't reply. Instead, she stood up, tucked her long black hair behind her right ear, and looked from Flynn to whoever stood behind him and back to Flynn again.

As Flynn directed his senses behind him, he noticed the heat from what must have been a fire. It warmed his back right thigh and smelled of burning coals. In a different situation it might have offered comfort. But in a dark and sweaty dungeon, it sent anxiety buzzing through his stomach.

When a hand grabbed the bottom of Flynn's shirt, he twisted to try to escape it. The wooden frame of the stock rattled at the hinges. He couldn't move.

The hand lifted his shirt and the heat from the fire pressed against Flynn's bare skin over his right kidney. It felt like the hand wore a thick rubber glove.

A look at Mistress and Flynn saw the concentration on her face as she watched the person behind him. Her tongue protruded slightly from her mouth as if it took focus to simply observe the man. As if she lived every step of it with him.

"What the fuck is he doing back there?" Flynn said.

A glance down at him, but Mistress quickly looked away as if fearful of missing something.

When Mistress flinched, Flynn nearly shouted at her again. But before he could speak, a searing pain lit up his right kidney. "Arghhhhhhhhhhhhhhhhh!"

Whatever they burned him with, the man behind kept the pressure on. No matter how Flynn moved, he couldn't escape the scorching press of it. It sent the pain of a thousand hard pinches into him.

The hiss of his burning flesh called through the room. A

second later, Flynn smelled the fatty charring of his own skin.

Still watching events behind him, Mistress' expression shifted from pain to pleasure and back again.

Flynn couldn't take anymore, but the hot pain kept on. His stomach bucked and he vomited bile all over the floor in front of him. Woozy as he fought to remain conscious, his legs wobbled and they threatened to give out beneath him.

The man behind him finally pulled the hot metal away and Flynn fell limp. Were it not for the stock, he would have collapsed on the ground.

The world in front of Flynn blurred through his tear-glazed eyes, and his wrists and neck hurt from where the stock took his body weight.

After he'd spat the acidic taste of bile away from him, Flynn's sight cleared a little and he looked at Mistress. "I'm going to cut your fucking throat."

She shook her head at him and replied in a calm and even tone, "No, you're not, sweetie. Besides, at the moment, you couldn't even tie your own shoelaces. You'd do well to remember who's in control here."

Even with the metal pulled away, Flynn's back remained on fire. It turned his entire body electric like every nerve ending had been exposed.

As Flynn started to lose consciousness again, Mistress grabbed his face in a hard pinch and pulled it up so he had to look at her. She gripped so tightly his teeth cut into the insides of his cheeks.

Just a few centimetres separated them when she said, "We're going to fill the wound with ash now so you don't bleed everywhere. Then we'll take you back to the prison."

Mistress pulled away, letting Flynn's head fall limp. She leaned over the stock, shoving her crotch in his face. When she pulled back, she had two iron brands. She showed them to Flynn, holding them so close he could smell his own seared flesh on the end of them.

"Sixteen," she said. "A one and a six. It's so people know who you are. We have to wait for eighteen, nineteen, and twenty. Then we can get on with it."

In too much pain to reply, Flynn stared at the bitch in front of him. She'd get hers; he'd fucking make sure of it.

Chapter Eighteen

The hood over Flynn's head blinded him as a hard and impatient hand shoved him forward. Each forceful push into the centre of his back made him stumble, his stomach lurching in anticipation of a trip. And with his hands bound, he'd be powerless to cushion the fall.

Yet somehow he managed to remain upright. He'd teetered on the brink of falling a few times, but he hadn't toppled over. Not yet at least.

One of the guards put a pincer grip on the back of Flynn's neck and it took all he had not to fold beneath the sharp sting of it.

When Flynn stopped still, the guard let go.

The crack of a bolt snapped free and Flynn jumped where he stood. Suddenly a rough hand grabbed his bound wrists, slipped a knife under the cable tie holding them together, and ripped the blade up, freeing his hands.

The guard behind him then pushed where he'd been branded, igniting the fire in his back again as he shoved him into the prison.

A sure sign of weakness in front of the other prisoners, Flynn yelped, stumbled from the shove, and crashed down, smashing his knees against the hard ground.

As he removed his hood, the gate slammed shut behind him. The bolt cracked home and they were locked in again.

Not that he recognised the prisoners in the room from his brief time in the dingy space earlier, but it looked like the same people still in there. They all stared at Flynn. He looked where number fifteen had lain dead. He'd gone now. Unfortunately, the brute who'd killed him hadn't.

"What the fuck are you looking at?" the large bully demanded as he loomed over Flynn.

Where Flynn had previously thought the dungeon smelled of body odour, he now recognised the tang of seared flesh. They all stank of it.

In no state to fight because of the pain of his brand, Flynn dropped his eyes to the dark ground, the flickering light from the torches in the walls doing little to illuminate the place.

Flynn shuffled out of the man's way and only looked up at him when he'd reached the wall at the other side of the space. He'd obviously done enough to placate him because he no longer seemed interested.

Now Flynn had returned to the prison, he saw something in the faces of the other prisoners. It took for him to be branded to identify the smell of the place, and now he looked at the sad faces around him, he connected to them because of the pain in his lower back. All of them had been marked like animals. He didn't need to see the burns to know that. They wore their scars in their stares.

The atmosphere in the prison seemed to boil just below the surface. Regardless of how long they'd all been there, a pecking order existed with the brute firmly at the top.

So when a skinny man walked over to Flynn, his ratty eyes narrowed to slits, he knew he couldn't back down again. Too much subservience and he'd go the way of fifteen.

"You're in my space, boy," the man said as he looked down at Flynn.

Aware of everyone else looking at him too, including the brute, Flynn got to his feet. Because of the pain in his back, he had to push off the wall to stand up.

Several breaths when he'd gotten upright to ride out the sharp pain over his kidneys, and Flynn found a little more resolve.

One last check to be sure everyone, including the brute, were watching, and Flynn said, "Now, I'm going to give you one chance."

The skinny man laughed. "One chance for what? You're in *my* space."

Flynn flashed his fist across the man's chin, putting a right cross square on him. The wet *clop* of it rang through the space before the man's legs folded and he crumpled to the ground.

Adrenaline sent heavy breaths through Flynn and he looked at the others as he rode it out. His hand ached from where he'd just dropped the skinny man, but he kept his fist balled anyway. The staring eyes of only a few seconds ago had vanished. Each person minded their own business again. Even the brute looked away.

Chapter Nineteen

Fuck knew how long had passed. Every time Flynn tried to get comfortable, either the cold and hard prevented it, or the fierce pain in his back screamed in agony. As electric as ever, his wound ran a constant angry buzz through him.

"Nicely handled."

Flynn looked to his right to see the blonde girl had snuck up close to him. A glance at the other prisoners and no one else seemed to be watching. He might not have had much experience beyond his community, but he knew one of the best ways to disarm a man often came in the form of a beautiful lady. At first he didn't reply, staring into the girl's eyes as he looked for deceit.

"I think you showed them you wouldn't be fucked with." She spoke in a whisper so only Flynn heard her. "More importantly, you showed *him* you wouldn't be fucked with." While looking at the large man in the middle of the prison, she added, "After his alpha-male display, he needed to see that."

At a guess, Flynn would have put the woman in her early twenties. The figure of someone still in her physical prime, she looked tired in her face, dark bags swollen beneath her eyes.

"Thanks," he finally said. "I would have rather not done it though."

The man he'd knocked out had woken up about ten minutes ago and scurried over to the other side of the prison. If any of the other prisoners were looking for a weak link, they weren't looking at Flynn anymore.

After she'd glanced around the place as if checking to make sure they didn't have an audience, the girl said, "No, but you *had* to do it."

Despite years of living with naked flames for illumination, Flynn still hadn't gotten used to how the flickering light animated the inanimate. One second the people around seemed to be closing in in his peripheral vision; the next they were farther away than ever.

"I'm One," the girl said as he held her hand out to Flynn.

"Sixteen," Flynn said back, wincing at another sharp kick from his wound when he stretched over to her.

"I know you are. And it fucking hurts, doesn't it?"

Flynn nodded at the second comment. "Although, I think I would have rather just had a one branded into me."

A raised eyebrow and One nodded. "Sure, but it also means I've been here longer than anyone else."

"How long?"

One shrugged in the low light. "A fortnight," she said, "maybe a month."

"A *month*?"

"Maybe."

Before Flynn could ask her anything else, the lock on the dungeon's door snapped free. The guards shoved two people in and announced them to the room. "Eighteen and nineteen. One more and it's party time, fuckers."

The two newest arrivals—two women who couldn't have weighed any more than about nine stone between them—stumbled into the room. They withdrew from the collective attention as if the stares caused them physical discomfort.

After a look at the glowering brute, they moved to the other side of the space. The poor fuckers had no idea of the pain that would come to them soon. What Flynn had seen as hostility in everyone's stares when he'd first arrived, he now saw as pity. They all knew what those two would have to face.

Once the room had settled down, Flynn said, "So what happens at twenty?"

Although One looked at him, she didn't reply.

"I thought you might have worked it out by now," he said, "being here for as long as you have."

One shrugged. "They don't tell you much down here."

Flynn shifted against the pain of his burn.

"What I can tell you," she said, "is the person who runs this place is a complete fucking lunatic."

"He is?"

"*She*," she said. "*She*. And yes, she's fucking insane."

Tired, in pain, and sweating from the heat of the room, Flynn closed his eyes and leaned his head against the hard wall behind him. It had been a long fucking day. After he let out a deep sigh, any desire to continue talking left him.

Chapter Twenty

One and Flynn hadn't spoken since he'd closed his eyes. And maybe he would have remained that way were it not for the *snap* of the lock on the prison cell's door. He opened his eyes to watch four guards walk in, much like they'd done with him. Although, they didn't kick either Eighteen or Nineteen in the face. He nearly said something as he watched the guards drag the women to their feet and lead them out, but what could he say. A 'fuck you' to the guards wouldn't have achieved much other than another kick in the face and he didn't want to see the women hurt like he'd been.

After the guards had left and locked the door behind them, Flynn felt the collective empathy in the place. They sat there like a group of people who'd been given some bad news. They were united in their solidarity for the afflicted. They were nervous for what would happen to the women.

A look at the primate in the middle and Flynn froze to see the brute staring straight at him. For a second he held his glare. The bullying man then looked from him to One and back to him again.

To save the stand-off, Flynn turned his attention to One. She sat hunched over, her arms hooked over her knees and her back arched. He spoke so only she heard him, painfully aware of the brute's attention as his glare bored into him. "So, if you don't know what happens when we reach twenty, how do you know about the woman who runs this place?"

"I used to live in a nearby community. Sure, we knew fucked-up shit was happening here, but we did our best to avoid knowing what that was. They left us alone. That was all we cared about. Until …"

A glance at the brute, who continued to watch them, and Flynn said, "Until?"

"Until they decided to take us over."

"How many did you have in your community?"

"Just shy of fifty."

"Where are the others now?"

One stared into the middle distance with glazed eyes as she said, "Dead. She slaughtered the lot of them."

"How come she didn't kill you?" Flynn looked at the brute again. The Neanderthal seemed ready to walk over.

"I've thought about that. I've had a lot of time to think. My only guess is that she wants someone to keep her legend alive. At least one witness needs to survive for people to understand just how fucking horrible she is. That's how it works, isn't it? Let the story spread. Once fear infects someone's mind, you've beaten them already, right?"

Flynn looked at the brute again. "What did she do to your community?"

One looked at Flynn, her eyes wide. "You *really* want to know?"

Flynn shrugged.

After a deep breath, One stared back into the middle distance. She looked detached from her words and spoke in a monotone. "She killed the children first. We had a village hall, which she forced everyone into. It had a stage."

It took several breaths before One spoke again, tears running down her face as she relived the experience. "She made the children line up on the stage, got them all singing a song they knew, and then …" She lost it for a second and dropped her head. A slight shake ran through her, and even in the poor light, Flynn watched her tears fall to the ground.

Another look at the brute and Flynn saw the smile on his twisted face.

One spoke again. "She cut their throats one by one."

"My *god*!" Flynn said. "We had a woman like that near us. It was about ten years ago now."

"Maybe it was the Queen."

"The *what*?"

"That's what she calls herself. After she'd killed the children, she dragged me out of the crowd and took me outside the village hall. She got her guards to nail every exit shut and then made me …" One lost it again and Flynn didn't push her. She'd tell him in her own time.

Chapter Twenty-One

The sound of approaching guards ran up the tunnel towards the prison and everyone in the room turned to face them, including One, who looked up from her grief. They opened the door and shoved Eighteen and Nineteen back into the room. They hadn't bound their hands like they had with Flynn, but they both had sacks over their heads.

The two women both fell to the ground as they came in. They brought the reek of seared flesh with them.

After they'd moved into a dark corner like beaten dogs, they huddled together and sobbed. The other prisoners paid them no mind. Not even the brute, who continued to stare over at Flynn and One with the same antagonising smile on his smug face.

About ten minutes had passed since One last spoke. She stared at Eighteen and Nineteen like everyone else did until the sadness had left her eyes. A steely glare replaced it and she straightened her back. "She made me set fire to the hall with all the people of my community inside. I *promise* you, Sixteen, when I get a chance, I'm going to make the cunt pay."

"So what's this, then?" The booming voice of the brute cut

through the room and Flynn's shoulders tensed at the sound of it. It had to come sooner or later.

The brute stepped forward a couple of paces. "It looks to me like we have a couple of lovebirds here. The first dungeon romance maybe?"

Both Flynn and One kept their mouths shut.

"You'll have to give me time to buy a new suit before you two tie the knot." He'd now stepped close enough for Flynn to see the glint in his dark eyes. The kind of arsehole that needed to dominate to feel secure. "And maybe let me have a go on it"—he nodded at One—"before you make an honest woman of her?"

One recoiled at the comment and Flynn got to his feet, his fists clenched, his heart pounding. The brute might have been bigger than him, but he'd already seen what Flynn could do when backed into a corner.

The brute laughed, his deep voice calling out into the tunnel beyond the dungeon. "What? You think you have the beating of *me*?"

Instead of replying, Flynn looked around at the other prisoners. Other than the man he'd knocked out, all of them huddled in groups of two to four people. The brute followed his line of sight.

"You'd do well to see you've isolated yourself," Flynn said. "Now I don't know what's waiting for us when we get to twenty, but I wouldn't mind betting most people are looking for an excuse to take you down if they get it."

The confidence visibly left the brute and his entire frame sank. Before he could offer a comeback, Flynn said, "Now, I'd fuck off back to your space in the middle of the room if I were you. You ain't welcome anywhere else."

Although he kept his fists clenched and his jaw locked tight, the brute shook his head and stepped back a pace. More for the theatrics of it than anything, he pointed one of his sausage fingers at Flynn. "You're on thin ice, boy. Thin fucking ice."

Flynn sat down and leaned against the wall. No need to goad the arsehole any further. One shuffled even closer to him and said, "Thanks, Sixteen."

"Flynn."

She smiled. "Thanks, Flynn. I'm Rose."

"Pretty name."

The crack of the lock might have spared her blushes. Just a shame that it came with the guard announcing, "Twenty," to the room as he shoved another prisoner in. Rose looked at Flynn, her features slack.

"Fuck," Flynn said. "I'm guessing we'll find out what happens next, then."

Chapter Twenty-Two

Because he'd been underground for so long, when the guards drove the prisoners out of the dungeon, Flynn couldn't see for the first few seconds. The glare burned his eyes and the heat instantly made him sweat. It felt even hotter above ground than in the heady prison.

Every step Flynn took reminded him of the pain covering his right kidney. The slightest jolt shook the swollen flesh around the wound. It made his back feel fat where it never had before. He'd also picked up a whole host of aches and pains from where he'd sat on the hard ground for hours.

Flynn heard it the second he walked out of the dungeon, but he still couldn't see well enough to make out the crowd and their purpose. They were obviously there to witness some kind of spectacle. A spectacle that the prisoners would be at the centre of.

As his sight recovered, Flynn frowned to look at the scene before him. The dungeon had been underground—that much he'd worked out—but now they'd exited it, he saw the deep pit that had been dug to access it. It looked like a huge square had been carved into the ground. Steep walls of exposed earth on three sides stood at least thirty metres tall. The only way out looked to be the long, slick slope in front of them. It led from where they were, all the way up to the crowd at the top about thirty metres above. Unless they wanted to turn around and walk back into the prison, they had just one option out of there.

Like Flynn, all of the prisoners had stopped and rubbed their eyes as they took in their surroundings. When the guards growled behind them, Flynn turned to see all of them waving bats to spur the prisoners forward.

As he slowly moved on, Flynn looked at the people above. At least a hundred spectators, maybe more, they'd all gathered around the vast pit and stared down at the prisoners. They were so far away, he struggled to see their facial expressions, but the jeers and cries said it all. They expected to be entertained, and they expected blood.

A look across at Rose and Flynn saw her staring up at the people too.

The pit must have taken months to dig without machinery. Months and an army of people. But they'd had twenty years since Vicky helped release the plague, and with very little incentive to travel—especially when the diseased fuckers wandered about—what else could people do?

As they were forced closer to the slope, Flynn screwed his nose up at the stench. He looked to either side of him and noticed the other prisoners doing the same. The large and wide incline looked slick from a distance, but now he'd drawn closer to it, Flynn saw what he'd perceived as wet mud to be something entirely different. Not only would the sewage be hard to climb, but he'd have to stop himself vomiting on the way up.

At the bottom of the hill, pointing up in the direction of the slick slope, were a militant line of wooden stakes. Each one looked as sharp as an arrow and they were thick enough to withstand bodies sliding into them. Blood stained their shafts. Not everyone would make it up the slope without sliding back into the stakes. The audience above seemed to be counting on it.

None of the prisoners spoke as they all moved through the line of stakes to the bottom of the slick hill. Sewage pooled from where it had run down the slope, coating the bottom of Flynn's shoes. A froth sat on the brown liquid, and the smell hung so heavy it damn near made his eyes water.

Another look at Rose and Flynn properly took in her form for the first time in the bright light. Skinny from where she'd spent the longest time of all the prisoners in the dungeon, she already looked weak. They must have fed her something, but it didn't look like much. Many of the other prisoners appeared the same. Even the brute seemed less brutish in the sun's strong glare. Where he'd come across as big and powerful in the shadows of the prison, he now looked overweight and unfit. If he needed more than strength, he'd surely find himself lacking.

Before Flynn could think on it any further, one of the guards shimmied through the filthy and bloody stakes. To see her tied a knot in his guts. Mistress!

She still wore her bloody leather apron as she walked up and down in front of the prisoners, a wide strut as if to accommodate her ample frame. She raised her voice, clearly for the large crowd who'd fallen silent above. "Ladies and gentlemen—and I ain't talking to you *dogs*," she said to the prisoners. "Please meet the newest line of hopefuls. We like to start with twenty, but as you all already know, number fifteen and seventeen didn't make it out of the dungeon. Anyone with those numbers should have received new ones by now."

When Flynn looked at the brute, he saw him straighten his back and lift his chin. He seemed proud that number fifteen hadn't made it.

"And now, numbers one to twenty," she said to the prisoners, "you've probably guessed what you need to do."

Another look at the huge slick hill and Flynn gulped. He ran his eyes all the way up it to the onlookers at the top.

"And what if we say no?" a dark-skinned girl asked. She stood no taller than about five feet and looked so skinny she'd snap. Although why she felt the need to shout out baffled Flynn. She didn't need to worry; she'd scoot up the hill like a lizard over hot sand.

Mistress looked at one of the guards behind the girl and nodded. The guard—a large man with powerful arms—raised his wooden baton and cracked her across the back of the head with a *tonk.* The sound echoed around the pit and the girl's legs buckled beneath her. The guard then buried a large knife into the back of her skull.

Silence hung in the air for a few seconds before Mistress said, "Anyone else want to speak out?"

No one responded.

The guard who'd dropped the girl lifted her shirt up to reveal the infected number six.

"Number six is down," he called at the people above. Groans

and moans met his words, and paper ticker-taped down onto the slope and the prisoners.

The paper took an age to make it to Flynn, but when one landed nearby, he saw the number six on it.

"Now, as you can see," Mistress said as she walked up to one of the stakes and pushed against the sharpened tip of it with her finger, "not everyone will make it past the first obstacle."

The first obstacle? Flynn wanted to ask how many there were, but he kept his mouth shut and gulped, his throat dry from the heat.

"But for those who do," Mistress continued, "you'll be rewarded. The prize for the winner is a place in *our* community. You get to live like the rest of us. As for those who don't make it"—she shrugged—"thanks for participating, and thanks for the entertainment." For a few seconds, she focused on the dead number six, the pool of piss she lay in turning red as she bled into it.

Another look up and down the line and Flynn nodded to himself. He had the beating of most of the prisoners there. Unlike the others, he'd been well fed and well rested until that moment. Some of them looked on the verge of collapse already. Time in the prison hadn't served any of them well.

"So," Mistress said and clapped her hands together, "without further ado, let the contest begin."

The spectators whooped and hollered, sending a deafening swirl of noise down into the pit. Someone threw a rock and it hit the slope with a wet *squelch*!

Mistress waved a finger up at the crowd. "Not yet! Wait for me to get out of the way first. *Jesus.*"

The rock sat as large as a football. After he'd looked at it for a few seconds, Flynn looked up at the crowd again. How many more would be thrown down while they climbed?

Mistress walked back through the spikes and past the prisoners to join the other guards. She removed a baton from her belt and stood in line with her peers. Blood stained the end of her bat and she seemed to take great pleasure in showing the prisoners that as she held it aloft. "Just in case you don't feel like climbing, know we have ways to motivate you. Prisoners, get ready …

"Ten."

Flynn shuffled forward with the others to the bottom of the hill.

"Nine."

He looked at Rose, her face pale like she'd vomit at any moment.

"Eight."

Flynn watched the brute glance from side to side as if looking for the weak ones to take down.

"Seven."

A deep inhale of the shit-scented air.

"Six."

A man burst into tears next to Flynn.

"Five."

A girl no older than about fifteen threw up.

"Four."

Flynn clenched his jaw, his frantic heart threatening to unsettle his stamina.

"Three."

The crowd above seemed to lean over even further, every one of them gripped with silent anticipation.

"Two."

The top of the hill mattered. Nothing else. Just get to the top.

Chapter Twenty-Three

"One!"

A deep lungful of the heady reek around him and Flynn stepped onto the slope. He slipped off immediately.

Several of the lighter prisoners on either side of Flynn managed to stay on with their first attempt. Not that he carried a huge amount of extra weight, but like number six, they couldn't have been any more than five stone dripping wet. Malnourished, they moved up the slope on their spindly limbs like spiders.

On Flynn's second attempt, he leaned forward and planted his hands into the slope first. Shit oozed up between his fingers.

Flynn ignored the heave threatening to turn through him and brought his right foot up again. This time he stabbed his toe into the soft ground, made sure he had some purchase, and pushed off against it.

When he remained on the slope, Flynn repeated the process with his left foot.

The crowd above screamed and jeered, but Flynn kept his attention on the hill in front of him. The rancid and muddy reek of human waste smothered him. Not that he could do anything to change it. He shut it out as best as he could and pushed on.

A *thud* and *squelch* shook the ground above Flynn, a damp spray of sewage splattering the top of his head. When he looked up, he saw another rock had been hurled down from the crowd. Like the one thrown before it, the huge stone had fallen so far that its momentum buried half of it into the soggy slope.

Slow progress for the next few metres, Flynn got to the rock and reached up for it. He tested it by pulling to see if it came loose. His legs shook from trying to hold his position with the strength in his toes. The rock remained in place.

Once he'd climbed up and had both of his feet on the rock, Flynn looked behind him to see Rose down to his left. Shit coated her forearms and she climbed with her mouth spread wide from where she clearly tried to catch her breath. She looked to be in pain from both the physical exertion of the climb and the overwhelming stench she had to endure.

When Flynn looked back up the hill, he flinched to see one of the front-running prisoners hurtling down towards him after having slipped. Legs and arms flailing, the prisoner screamed and looked set to crash straight into him.

The crowd followed his fall with a loud and unified, "Wooooooooooooooooooooo …"

Fortunately for Rose, Flynn had checked her position beforehand. When the prisoner got close to him, he braced himself against the rock, took the impact of the man, and shoved him to his right, away from him and Rose.

The prisoner reached out to grab Flynn on his way past and

missed, his ratty face twisted with rage and fear.

Flynn recognised him as the man who'd squared up to him in the dungeon. Any guilt vanished as he thought about the way he'd behaved. Better to see him fall than any of the others. Well, the brute could have gone first and then him.

The ratty man gathered momentum and spun as he slid, his arms and legs swinging away from him. He caught one prisoner with a loud *clop*, and then another a second later. All three slid down the hill towards the spikes.

The crowd's shout increased in volume the closer they got to the bottom. "WooooooooOOOOOOO."

The three prisoners crashed into the stakes one after the other and the crowd erupted into cheers.

The ratty man took a spear to the face. It protruded through the back of his head and he hung limp from it.

One of the prisoners took two spears through their torso.

The third prisoner took one through the chest.

The one with the two spears twisted and moaned while the other two remained motionless. Dead.

Flynn looked over his left shoulder to see Rose staring up at him. She dipped a nod at him. He returned the gesture, his legs shaking from adrenaline and the effort of perching on the rock.

Chapter Twenty-Four

The crowd erupted again, but Flynn couldn't see why. Someone must have said something to them because they'd been whipped up into a frenzy. A bunch of giddy primates, they threw a meteor shower of rocks down at the prisoners.

Each rock landed with a squelch and threw shit into the air. Flynn closed his mouth as he felt the mess of it patter his face.

One of the final rocks to be hurled down spun as it fell. Flynn watched it land on top of a prisoner no more than a metre away from him, the ground shaking with the impact of it.

The size of a car's wheel, the rock pinned the prisoner's head into the muddy slope and turned him instantly limp.

Flynn looked at Rose again, her wide eyes a reflection of his own disbelief. They needed to get off the slope as soon as possible.

Chapter Twenty-Five

Still on his rock, the dead person still pinned to the slope next to him, Flynn remained stationary as he watched several of the prisoners pass him on their way up the steep hill. Although reluctance sat as a dead weight in his muscles, he couldn't stay there all day. One last check behind him and he saw Mistress walk over to the impaled prisoners on the stakes.

A wide strut, her leather apron hanging down in front of her, and Mistress shouted out, "Eight, twelve, and nineteen."

A section of the crowd booed and it snowed slips of paper for a second time.

The fierce dominatrix looked up the slope and at what Flynn assumed to be the body next to him. The sun must have been in her eyes because she squinted as she clearly tried to see better. When one of her guards handed her a pair of binoculars, she pressed them to her face. The shirt of the pinned prisoner had lifted at the back, revealing his number.

"Number three," Mistress called out.

A slightly quieter "Boo", and more slips of paper rained down.

At no more than five metres up the slope and with over four times that amount to go, Flynn looked up the hill again. No one in front of him looked like they'd slip. Not that he could predict it; he could only react when it happened. He had to keep going. Fuck knew what they'd do to him if he ended up as the last one to reach the top.

A mixture of exhaustion and fear shook Flynn's legs as he climbed. Sweat ran into his eyes, but he dared not wipe it away. Better to have eyes stinging from his sweat than rubbing the disease from a stranger's waste into them.

Every step Flynn took could be the one where he slipped. If that happened, the spikes would be the only things to stop him. He couldn't think like that though. Instead, he watched the slick ground and continued his climb. One step at a time, he stabbed his right toe into the mud, paused, and then repeated the process with his left.

The brute climbed on Flynn's right. Red-faced and sweating, he pulled himself up at a slow and steady pace.

A woman who looked to be in her thirties climbed just ahead of the thickset alpha male. Despite the size difference, he gained on her with each step. Where she had a slight frame and little body weight as her advantage, she looked like she struggled for stamina.

When the brute grabbed her ankle, Flynn gasped to watch him pull on it and drag her back.

The woman screamed on her way down and spun in circles. She flapped and slapped her hands against the ground as if it would slow her down. It sprayed up a wave of muddy water, but did little else.

Like the ratty man had, she clattered into a prisoner on her way to the bottom. The collision drove an "oomph" from one of them and they both hurtled towards the stakes.

Flynn flinched at each wet pop as the stakes impaled the two prisoners.

The crowd erupted again and Flynn saw the slightest smile on the brute's face.

"Ten and fourteen," Mistress called out and more paper fluttered down onto the slick hill as Flynn continued to climb.

Chapter Twenty-Six

By the time he'd reached the halfway point, Flynn's muscles were on fire. It felt like he'd been climbing for hours and he had to cover the same distance again before he reached the top. The heat had turned his throat dry, and every time he gulped, he tasted shit. Either the thick stench had flavoured the air, or some had gotten into his mouth during the climb. Probably the latter, not that it bore thinking about.

No one had slipped since the brute had dragged the woman back.

A look up the slope, the bright sun bouncing off the slick surface, and Flynn saw Rose about three-quarters of the way up.

But he had to focus on his own progress. A jab of his right toe into the muddy ground and he checked it for purchase. When satisfied, he pushed up, his leg shaking from the effort, and jabbed his left toe into the ground. Each push farther up the hill robbed a little more of his strength, but he kept going. He had to.

The first Flynn heard of the next person sliding down the hill came just a little bit too late. When he heard a wet *whoosh*, he looked up to see a spinning mess of limbs. A second later, it clattered into him.

The collision sent a sharp pain through Flynn's forearms first and then his shins as they wiped him out.

Just as Flynn lost control, he looked up to see Rose staring down the hill at him, anxiety twisting her features.

Chapter Twenty-Seven

Flynn lost sight of Rose's worried face as he joined the momentum of the sliding prisoner. He moved down the slope like a tea tray over ice, the slick surface rushing past him.

In the split second he had, Flynn quickly shoved away from the man who'd knocked into him. It altered his course slightly and pushed the man away too.

Flynn spun out of control, his arms and legs flailing away from his body with the momentum of his spin.

The wet rushing sound of the sewage grew louder and surrounded Flynn while the ground shook. Fuck knew how many rocks had been launched down at him, but they were still coming. Over the sound of the wet slope, he heard the crowd going crazy.

In an attempt to control the spin, Flynn tried to sit up. He lifted his head just about enough to see him: the prisoner who'd been crushed beneath the rock. He remained pinned to the slope like a dead butterfly in a glass case.

The sloppy ground kicked up from Flynn's feet and hit him as if fired from a muck spreader. The spatter of wet clumps clopped into his face and he pressed his mouth tightly closed.

Even with the onslaught of fecal matter, he kept his attention on his intended target. One chance. One chance to save his life.

Flynn reached out for the rock. He caught it, but only with his fingertips. Slick with shit, they slid straight from the rock's abrasive surface, the jagged stone sending streaks of fire where he made contact. It felt as if he'd sheared the tips of his fingers clean off.

However, it slowed him down just enough to give him time to grab the dangling legs of the pinned corpse.

His damp hands slid down the dead man's wet trousers, his fingertips throbbing from the pain of catching the rock.

Flynn squeezed harder, gripping on with all he had.

Just before he slipped from the bottom of the corpse's legs, he stopped with a jolt at the man's ankles.

Flynn exhaled hard and held on so tightly his arms ached.

Confident he wouldn't slip, Flynn looked down over his left shoulder to see the prisoner who'd clattered into him slide from the slope into the sharp stakes at the bottom.

The crowd cheered again as a stake popped through the man. It sounded like it shattered his ribcage.

While still holding on, Flynn listened to Mistress at the bottom of the slope. "Number thirteen!"

The crowd booed and slips of paper rained down.

A few seconds later, Flynn recovered his breath enough to do something more than just stay put. He looked back up the hill. He'd lost about half of the distance he'd climbed. He watched a couple of the front-runners, including Rose, climb the ledge at the top to safety. He couldn't do it. Then he looked down at number thirteen. "Come on, Flynn," he said to himself, "you don't have a choice."

Chapter Twenty-Eight

What felt like a lifetime had passed before Flynn reached the top of the slope. His entire body trembled from the effort of the climb. By the time he'd reached the halfway point, his limbs shook beyond control, but he kept his tense frame locked and inched up the hill, thinking only about the next step.

It had taken him so long, even the crowd had fallen silent as they watched him climb.

A sheer wall ran along the top of the hill. No more than two metres tall, it stood between Flynn and freedom. Or at least freedom from the shitty slope.

After Flynn reached up and grabbed the ledge, he looked down to check his footing and a stream of hot liquid rained down on him. Had he been more alert, he probably wouldn't have looked up again. Had he been more alert, he wouldn't have ended up staring at an exposed penis as one of the spectators pissed on him, half of the stale urine running straight into his eyes and mouth. Several more men stood on either side of the pissing man and then they too emptied their bladders on his head.

The crowd had picked back up again, and they whooped and hollered as if geeing the pissing men on.

Despite his rage sending his pulse hammering and winding his shoulders tight, Flynn could do nothing but take it. If he let go of the ledge to grab one of them, he might slide back down the slope. He'd remember the men and he'd make sure they paid when he got the chance. He'd make sure every one of the vicious fuckers in the fucked-up community paid. He spat on the ground several times, but it did nothing to rid his mouth of the taste of piss.

When the streams of urine stopped, Flynn looked up again to see the men put their shrivelled dicks away. Many of them stared down at him, sneering as if proud of what they'd just done. They'd get theirs. He'd make sure of it.

The men turned away to be replaced by one woman. She had a bucket in her grip. She appeared to be struggling under its weight. Flynn looked down just in time for the cold splash of it to hit the back of his head rather than his face.

From the smell, consistency, and what he saw of the bucket's contents before it slid down the hill, Flynn assumed it to be excrement, rancid animal guts, and some kind of rotten food. His stomach flipped in response to the acrid reek. A second later he vomited bitter-tasting bile on his shoes.

A shake of his head and Flynn spat again. "So this is what happens to the last one up the slope."

Despite the assault, Flynn kept his grip on the ledge. The ground had turned slicker beneath his feet because of all the liquid they'd poured on him. If he let go now, he'd be screwed.

A searing pain then burned through the back of Flynn's right hand. He managed to hold on and looked up at the woman who'd held the bucket. The words came out before he'd a chance to hold them back. "What the fuck?"

The woman hissed at him while twisting her foot. Much more and she'd break the bones in the back of his hand.

Before she could stamp on him again, a guard rushed up behind her. Flynn continued to hold onto the ledge but ducked.

The vicious woman screamed as she flew over the top of Flynn. She hit the slope hard enough for the impact to drive the air from her body. The sound of her shrill cry raced down the hill with her.

The woman's scream ended with a now familiar wet squelch. Flynn looked behind to see her impaled like the prisoners had been. He also saw rope ladders had been dropped down to Mistress and the guards, and they were currently climbing up one of the sheer walls to the top of the pit.

"That's not on," the guard shouted at the people as he pointed down the slope at the now dead woman. "They may be prisoners, but we *don't* cheat." He pointed his thick finger at Flynn. "He *deserves* to be here. From what I've just seen, he's more than earned it."

The crowd didn't respond, but they backed away as Flynn pulled himself up over the ledge. He couldn't see any of the other prisoners.

Just as Flynn opened his mouth to thank the guard, someone dropped a sack over his head and his world turned dark. Maybe his gratitude had come a little too soon.

Chapter Twenty-Nine

A rough grip clamped around Flynn's right bicep and stung where it clung on. Clearly one of the place's many guards, but fuck knew where he planned on taking him. It would serve no purpose to fight it. Not at that moment. He let the guard lead him wherever they were going.

After a few minutes of walking over what felt like a broken road—the long grass pushing up through its uneven surface—the acoustics of Flynn's surroundings changed. The path sloped downwards and both his and the guard's footsteps echoed off what sounded like the enclosed walls of a tunnel.

At a guess, Flynn would have said they walked about one hundred metres before the sound of his environment changed again. The echo stretched away from him where the enclosed space clearly opened up.

The grip on Flynn's right bicep eased and the guard behind him grabbed the top of the sack on his head before ripping it off.

Before Flynn found his bearings, a powerful rush of frigid water smothered him in an icy blast, forcing him to inhale hard.

Every muscle in his body snapped tight in reaction to the chill, and his pulse ran off the charts.

When Flynn tried to back away from the water—his arms folded protectively across his body—a pole of some sort jabbed straight into his brand and he arched his back in response. He rushed towards the icy assault again. The message seemed pretty clear: stay the fuck still and take it!

The aggressive and frigid soaking cleaned all the shit from Flynn's body and damn near ripped his skin off too. The chill wound him so tight he felt brittle.

The water stopped and the place fell silent. Flynn looked around. They were in the centre of what looked to be an underground car park. It looked like the kind of place that would have an old commercial building stretching above where they stood.

Several guards stared at Flynn and one of them threw a towel at him. It hit him in the face.

"Take those disgusting clothes off," the guard—a large man with broad shoulders, a bald head, and a sword in his hands—said.

Flynn stripped, threw his clothes down, wrapped the towel around himself, and tried to dry off as quickly as he could.

Thank god he had cropped hair; the sewage would have been a nightmare to get out were it any longer. No doubt they would have turned the hose on him for longer too.

Once Flynn had dried himself off, the same large guard picked some clothes up and threw them at him one item at a time. Briefs, tracksuit bottoms, and a T-shirt.

Flynn put all the clothes on.

Even though he'd gotten dressed, Flynn continued to shiver. They were far enough underground it made the June heat redundant.

For a few seconds, the guards—six of them in total—stared at Flynn and he stared back. So occupied with the motley crew in front of him, he didn't hear a guard approach from behind. He jumped as the whoosh of fabric turned his world dark again. By the smell of things, they'd used a different hood because any trace of shit had gone. Silver linings and all that.

Although the guard grabbed his right bicep like he had before, this time he used much less force. He led Flynn away from where he currently stood.

***

After about a minute and a few twists and turns, they came to a flight of stairs. The guard slowed down to allow Flynn to feel his way up without tripping.

The metal stairs clocked beneath Flynn's steps as they continued their climb. The cold had already left Flynn's bones. Sweat itched all over his body from both the exertion and the change in temperature as they scaled higher. Although only faint at that moment, he could hear the sound of people—another fucking crowd.

"Where are you taking me?" Flynn asked.

The guard gripped harder and shoved Flynn forward. He caught his foot on the next step and he would have tripped were it not for the guard holding onto him.

"Okay, okay, I get it. No more questions."

The grip eased and the guard slowed down again.

***

After another few minutes of climbing, Flynn's legs shook and he panted beneath his oppressive hood. The guard gave him a sharp tug to halt him and then walked past him.

What sounded like a metal handle snapped down in front of them. A moment later the sounds of the crowd raised in volume. They'd clearly just opened a door separating them and the spectators. Although, what they'd come to spectate, Flynn couldn't guess.

Before Flynn could think on it any further, the guard tugged him forward through the open doorway.

After several steps, a strong wind crashed into Flynn. Before he had time to think, the guard had walked around behind him again and ripped his hood away.

Flynn's stomach lurched and he instinctively stepped back a pace from the edge of the tall building. At least twenty storeys up, maybe more, he looked at the small people below. They all whooped and hollered at his arrival. It had to be the same crowd who'd watched him climb the hill.

A derelict town much like the one close to Home, Flynn looked out over it from his vantage point on top of an old tower block.

Now he'd stepped back from the edge, Flynn relaxed a little, the strong breeze cooling his sweating face. He looked to his right down the line of prisoners and saw what he assumed to be all of the ones who'd climbed the shitty hill successfully. They all wore the same clothes as him.

It took Flynn a few seconds, but when he saw Rose, he

relaxed a little and let go of a relieved sigh.

When Flynn looked at the guard behind him who'd led him up the stairs, his blood ran cold. A wide smile on her wicked face, Mistress stared back at him. She then walked past him and stood on the edge of the building, about to address the crowd. Whatever she had to say to them at that point, it wouldn't be good.

Chapter Thirty

Mistress paraded up and down in front of the line of prisoners and said nothing. Flynn's sight had fully adjusted to the bright glare of the sun and he now saw the glisten of fresh blood on her leather apron. Again. So slick, it shimmered like oil riding the top of a wave.

A wide and leering grin split Mistress' gaunt face. Her black hair danced in the wind and she moved with sure-footed steps. She firmly planted her weight down with each stride forward, the gravel on the rooftop crunching beneath her strut.

From the way Mistress looked at them, Flynn knew they existed on a knife edge. At any moment, she could send any one of them flying from the top of the building. They'd best recognise and respect that.

Despite walking right on the lip of the building, Mistress didn't seem in the least bit bothered about the fall. Clearly familiar with being up there, she owned the space. Flynn watched her and eased back a step. How many people had she launched from the top in the past?

To look at the vicious woman sent chills through Flynn, so

he looked at the abandoned town beyond instead. Like all of the other towns he'd visited, many of the buildings had fallen into disrepair. Maybe rats lived down there like in the town close to Home. Although probably not. He scanned the shadows regardless and looked for the movement of small bodies.

At least one hundred people gathered around the bottom of the tower block and stared up. Flynn had to shield his eyes from the sun to see all their gawking faces. The hot June day pressed down on him, and despite the strong breeze, Flynn sweated in his T-shirt and joggers.

The town didn't look like home for the people, and no matter where Flynn looked, he couldn't see any signs of either fortification or dwellings. Maybe he'd find out where they lived if he won the stupid competition.

When Mistress shouted at the prisoners, it snapped Flynn from his musings and he jumped.

"Right," she screeched like a cawing bird, "we need to know your numbers. One by one, I'd like you to step forward and tell the good people down below what your number is. We need to make sure the people with skin in the game know who they're rooting for."

A skinny girl with matted hair stepped forward. She looked to be barely out of her teens and her voice wobbled as she shook and said, "Hi—"

"Louder!" Mistress yelled and stamped a black-booted foot against the gravel roof of the building.

"Hi!" the girl shouted to the people below. "I'm Samantha—"

In two steps, Mistress rushed at the girl and leaned into her face. She shouted so loud Samantha pulled back as if from the force of it. "I don't give a fuck what your name is. What *number* are you, sweetheart?"

Samantha flushed red and stammered for a few seconds. "N-number … number five. I'm number five."

When Mistress spun her finger at the girl, Samantha turned around. She lifted her T-shirt to show the crowd her number five over her right kidney. The angry red wound looked a long way from healed, the glisten of pus turning it shiny.

If the permanent throb of his brand gave him any indication, Flynn's probably looked as bad. Or would when it got as old and infected as Samantha's had.

A few seconds passed where neither Mistress nor Samantha spoke, but Mistress glared at the young girl as if she would cave her skull in at any moment.

As much as Flynn wanted to tell the girl to step back, he wouldn't put his neck on the line for her.

Samantha finally got the hint and moved back into line with the others.

It took a few more seconds for Mistress to move on and stare at Rose. Flynn's heart beat faster and he balled his fists. Would he step in if he needed to?

"Hi," she called down to the people. "I'm number one." Some of the crowd cheered as she spun around and showed them the brand over her left kidney. Clearly the people with a number one ticket. She promptly stepped back into line.

"Quite the confident one, aren't we?" Mistress said, but Rose didn't respond.

Each prisoner stepped forward at Mistress' request, repeating the same routine Rose had laid down for them. Flynn paid extra attention when they came to the brute.

Although overweight, the thickset ginger man wore strength in his heavy frame. Farmer strength rather than athlete strength, he looked like he could break bones. The wind tossed his fine ginger hair as he stepped forward and looked at the people down below. "I'm number seven."

A small section of the crowd responded to his number with cheers and shouts.

The ego of the brute seemed to drive him and would no doubt get him into trouble. Unlike the other prisoners, he remained a step ahead of the line and glared at Mistress. Almost an open challenge to the woman, it took for her to tilt her head to one side in an avian twist for him to turn around, reveal the number seven over his right kidney, and step back.

Mistress watched him like she'd peck his eyes out. If only she'd throw him off the roof. She then looked at the next prisoner, who stepped forward, introduced herself, and stepped back quicker than any of the others had as if to make up for the brute's faux pas.

By the time Mistress got to Flynn on the end of the line, he'd grown so nervous his stomach clamped and he felt nauseated. He stepped forward and called down, "Sixteen," to the people below before turning around and showing them his right kidney. He stepped back into line with the others.

Like she had with the brute, Mistress stared at Flynn as if contemplating her next move. She then pointed at him and his legs shook. If he made a break for it, how far would he get before someone took him out? Surely there had to be guards waiting just behind the metal door to the stairs.

"One," Mistress said and moved onto the person next to him. "Two, three, four, five …" She paused, the strong wind rocking her where she stood, and stared at the brute. "Six, seven, eight, nine."

Samantha stood at the end of the line, skinny and still shaking. Mistress hadn't counted her yet.

Another twist of her head and Mistress said, "Well, well."

It happened so quickly, Flynn nearly missed it.

In one fluid movement, the vicious woman lurched forward, grabbed Samantha's forearm, dragged her towards the edge of the building and said, "Ten's my unlucky number," as she threw her off.

The poor girl screamed all the way down, and Flynn—like the others—stepped forward to watch her hit the ground. The crowd parted in time for her to connect with the concrete with a deep *crack*. Her body fell instantly limp and lay as a twisted approximation of a human form, her limbs bent and buckled in ways that shouldn't be possible.

As one, the prisoners all stepped back from the edge of the building again. They all moved a little farther away than they'd stood before and watched Mistress with wide, fearful eyes. When Flynn looked across, he saw shock even on the brute's face.

Chapter Thirty-One

"Now," Mistress called out as she walked along the edge of the building's roof again. She stamped a foot down with each word. "Now, now, now, now, now." When she reached the brute, she stopped.

The thickset ginger man clenched his jaw, pulled his shoulders back, and raised his chin. Not quite as defiant since poor Samantha had been launched from the roof, but a clear show of strength nonetheless. It told Mistress he wouldn't go down as easily as Samantha had.

It felt like the longest time as Mistress said nothing; she simply stared at him. "You want to follow her, do you?" she finally said.

The large red-headed man didn't say no. He most certainly didn't say yes either. It would have been much better if she'd thrown him off instead of Samantha—and she still could. The brute finally lowered his stare, subservient enough to appease her.

A tittering laugh and Mistress moved away. As she spoke, she threw wide and flowing arm movements. Theatrics that probably had an effect for the people down below, but looked ridiculous to Flynn so close to her. She spoke for the benefit of the crowd. "The people down there need to know who you fuckers are."

Each footstep slammed down on the edge of the roof as if challenging the decrepit building's stability. "You," she said and stopped in front of a man no taller than about five feet seven inches. When she moved close to him, she dwarfed him. "Who are you, little fella?"

Mistress stood aside so the man could step forward. Whilst wringing his hands, he looked down at the people and said, "I'm number two."

"Not your number, you moron. What's your name?"

"J—"

Before he could get his name out, Mistress grabbed him by his T-shirt and pulled him to the very edge of the roof. She pointed down at the crowd. "Tell *them*."

"Jake," he shouted, his eyes closed as he shook and cried. "My name's Jake Schwartz."

"Anyone got number two?" Mistress called down to the people, her now familiar lear twisting her vicious face.

A group in the crowd cheered in response like they had the first time each of the prisoners revealed their numbers.

Mistress stepped away from the man, looked him up and down, and turned back to the people below, shouting as she said, "I don't fancy yours much."

The crowd laughed. Although the small section who'd cheered didn't. Their horse wouldn't be coming in today.

A strong pat on his back and Jake thrust his arms out to the sides to prevent himself from falling. "So, J-Jake Schwartz," Mistress said, "tell us where you're from. All the people with a number two may win extra food rations if you win, so tell them a little bit about yourself. Help them connect with you so at least it matters to someone when your pathetic life is snuffed out."

Still with his eyes closed, Jake spoke rapid words. "I left a community about twenty miles away. We only had a few people there and I wanted to meet someone. Thought I could maybe find love."

Mistress' laugh boomed like thunder. "Wow." She looked at Jake and laughed again, her face red, her eyes tearing up with her mirth. "How fucking romantic. Although it would seem— even at the end of the world—that the diminutive Jake Schwartz *still* can't get laid."

The crowd laughed again.

Before Jake could say anything else, Mistress shoved him backwards. He tripped and fell on his arse, some of the gravel kicking up around him.

Because Flynn had his attention on the fallen Jake and watched him get to his feet, he only saw Mistress had gone to Rose when she said, "You! Step forward."

Flynn's heart flipped to watch Rose move away from the line. Quick enough so she didn't need Mistress' help, she walked right to the edge of the building. A strong gust of wind and she'd fall.

"I'm Rose," she said to the crowd. "I'm number one and I used to belong to a community that got taken down a month or two back."

Not a lie, but she didn't blame the Queen. The wind picked

up and Flynn's heart fluttered to watch Rose rock on the edge of the building.

For a short while, Mistress said nothing. She moved close to Rose and stared at her as if contemplating her fate. She then turned to the crowd. "Who has number one?"

The cheer for Rose rang louder than it had for Jake. It didn't look like she had any more people in her crowd than he had in his. The louder noise simply showed more confidence in their champion.

"Quite the fan club, it would seem," Mistress said. After she'd looked Rose up and down, she added, "I can see why." Instead of shoving her, she shooed her back by waving her hand at her.

Rose glanced at Flynn on her way back into line.

The thud of Mistress' steps hit the roof again as she walked down the edge of it. Each step drew closer to Flynn. A fierce scowl as she looked at each prisoner until she finally stopped in front of him. "And here he is, the survivor. The one who should have died, but somehow made it up shit hill. Step forward, honey."

Flynn didn't challenge her, his pulse racing as he stepped to the edge of the roof. To look down at the people far below made his stomach lurch and his already weak legs wobbled. "My name's Flynn," he called out, loud enough to make his dry throat itch. Sweat rose on his brow and ran down his face. "I'm number sixteen."

In what seemed to be her theatrical fashion, Mistress held the bottom of her chin and watched Flynn. "And tell us where you're from, sweetheart."

"Biggin Hill."

"The what now?"

"Biggin Hill," Flynn said and looked down at the dead Samantha. He lost his words for a second before he said, "I went there with my parents and their friend when the plague started. We found high ground and waited it out."

"And where are the others now?"

Flynn sighed as he said it. "Dead."

"Wow, I should start calling you lucky from now on."

The crowd laughed, but Flynn didn't respond as the pain of Vicky's death burned through him. He'd dealt with his parents' passing, but since Serj had told him how Vicky had died, it had pulled up what he'd previously believed to be processed emotions.

At that moment, Mistress placed a hand in between Flynn's shoulder blades. A firm enough pressure to show him his life belonged to her now. One shove and he'd fall. "Who has number sixteen?"

The loudest cheer yet.

"They like you, sweetheart."

Flynn looked down at the people as they continued to shout and cheer.

"I suppose they saw what you did on poo hill. No one's fallen that far and still made it. Maybe there *is* something about you." Mistress then applied a little more pressure to Flynn's back.

Flynn pushed his toes into the roof against her gentle shove, her press getting harder with each passing second and the gravel slipping beneath his feet.

When the pressure got to the point just before Flynn could

fall, Mistress let go and he stumbled backwards.

Once Flynn had pulled far enough away from the edge, he let a relieved sigh go. He could feel Rose looking at him, but he didn't look back. Instead, he watched Mistress turn to the crowd and bow, leaning out over the edge of the roof as if she had no fear of falling. Of course he wanted to push her off at that point, but it wouldn't serve any purpose. They wouldn't get through the metal door behind them before they were overwhelmed by guards.

As if reading his thoughts, the sound of footsteps approached from behind. Before Flynn could look around, someone pulled yet another hood over his head. It turned his already sweating face hotter. The thick fabric and the heat of the day combined to turn the air in his dark space so heavy he struggled to breathe.

When the guard behind Flynn pulled him back towards the stairs, some of the tension left his body. Fuck knew where they planned on taking them next, but at least they weren't throwing him off the roof like poor Samantha.

Chapter Thirty-Two

The rattle of metal against metal clattered through the prison. It took a hold of Flynn's already frayed nerves and electrocuted them, waking him from his uncomfortable sleep.

Not only did Flynn have a headache and a backache, but he had such sore muscles he doubted if he'd be able to travel far. It took slow and tentative movements, but he unfurled himself from Rose.

Mistress stopped hitting the bars with her baton and opened the cell door.

Despite how many times he'd heard locks opening on large doors over the years, Flynn still hadn't gotten used to the sound. The crack of the bolt snapped through him—a sharp reminder of his incarceration.

Mistress stormed into the prison, her heavy boots slamming down against the hard linoleum floor. The way her apron glistened in the light suggested she had yet more fresh blood on her.

"Get up, you lazy fucks," Mistress boomed and kicked one of the prisoners. The woman yelped from the blow.

"By the end of the day," Mistress continued, "there will only be one of you left. We don't have much room in our community, so you need to prove you're worthy of the spot."

Flynn managed to sit up by the time Mistress drew close, so he avoided her kick. His brand throbbed and it felt as if the infection had gotten worse overnight. How long before he got blood poisoning from it?

They'd spent the night in an abandoned jail cell in an abandoned police station. A hard linoleum floor was covered in grit and dust, but at least they weren't put in that cursed damp dungeon again. They remained in the town they'd been in the previous day. The town that the people surely didn't live in, but it served as a good place to host their sick games.

Early the previous evening, when they'd first been locked up, Flynn and Rose had spoken to one another. But the brute and the guards told them to shut the fuck up very quickly, so they did. As the night drew on and it got darker inside the cell, they moved close to each other for comfort. By the time they'd both fallen asleep, they were wrapped around one another as if holding on for dear life.

Rose got to her feet first, seemingly nimble despite what they'd been through the previous day. Her blonde hair sat wild and out of control. It reminded Flynn of straw—not that he'd tell her that. She pulled a tight-lipped smile at him and held her hand in his direction.

Flynn took her surprisingly strong grip and let her pull him to his feet. She'd been a rock for him over the past day; she must want something in return.

Mistress didn't say anything else, but she stalked around the cell, walking close to each person as she held onto the metal baton she'd used to wake them with. The non-verbal threat did enough to force all nine prisoners into a line.

Chapter Thirty-Three

Instead of leading the prisoners out the front door, Mistress took them up several flights of stairs within the building. They must have travelled three, maybe four storeys up.

At the top of the stairs, Mistress kicked a door so hard it broke off its hinges and clattered down to reveal another roof beyond it. The bright summer sunshine flooded in and Flynn recoiled from the glare but continued walking.

On the roof of the police station, the heat made Flynn sweat and he gulped against his dry throat. The last water he'd tasted had been when they'd hosed him down, and he'd only taken a mouthful then.

It took several blinks for Flynn's vision to clear. When it did, he wished it hadn't. His stomach lurched to look at the sight before him and he muttered, "Fuck."

Maybe he'd said it a little too loudly because Rose turned to look at him before she looked back at what lay ahead of them.

A thick rope had been anchored against the edge of the police station's roof. It had been stretched taut across a gap of about twenty metres to a building on the other side of the street. Rings hung down from it at regular intervals. Each ring hung from a length of rope about a metre long. If they wanted to get across, they'd have to swing from one ring to the next.

The crowd from the previous day had returned. If anything, there looked to be more people than before. Flynn did a double take when he saw a large chair amongst the press of bodies. A woman sat on it. She looked to be in her forties, had a slim figure, shiny black hair, and a pretty face. Pretty in an objective sense. Pretty like a vase could be pretty. Pretty like a statue. He saw nothing attractive about her. Nothing at all.

Before he could look at the woman for any longer, Mistress shouted at the prisoners, loud enough for the crowd below to hear. "Well, my lovelies," she said. "This is your next challenge." She walked to the edge of the police station's roof and looked down. She tapped the stretched rope with her foot. "Not quite the drop you had yesterday from the office block, but enough to kill you. Especially when …"

Mistress didn't finish her sentence because she didn't need to. The squeak of large wooden cartwheels called out through the abandoned town. Flynn looked down to see a group of people move several carts into place. Each one looked like it had once been pulled by a tractor. Like something that had been used to move large bales of hay. Now they had stakes on them, much like the ones at the bottom of the shitty hill. The stakes pointed straight up and were sharpened into points. The carts and stakes were covered in bloodstains.

The now familiar grin split Mistress' witch face as she stared down at the people moving the carts. When one of them gave her a thumbs-up, she cackled and turned back to the prisoners.

"Nine of you left. Let's see how many there are by the time we get to the other building. Line up in numerical order."

When Rose glanced at Flynn, he reached out and touched her forearm. Only fleeting. He didn't need Mistress picking up on it. Any connection the prisoners had would be exposed and exploited for her sick pleasure.

The prisoners fell into line and Flynn ruffled his nose at the smell of flatulence from one of them. Nerves hung thick in the air.

"Right," Mistress shouted, her call echoing through the town. "We don't have all fucking day. You"—she pointed at Rose—"get on those fucking rings now."

Flynn looked at the bloodstained stakes on the carts then at the crowd and their expectant faces. He looked at the Queen amongst her servants. He looked at Mistress and her clear giddiness at what they were about to witness. Finally, he looked back at Rose.

Rose sat down on the roof and dangled her legs over the side. She reached down and pulled the first ring up to her. Her cheeks puffed from where she exhaled.

Flynn looked away as Rose slid from the roof. The crowd cheered and he stared at his feet. He couldn't watch.

Chapter Thirty-Four

Although Flynn didn't watch Rose, he might as well have. In fact, from the sounds the crowd made, it probably would have been better than trying to judge her progress based on their response. At least he would have seen the reality of it. Instead, he lived his own imagined horror for the entire crossing.

When the crowd cheered, Flynn looked up to see Rose climb through the window on the other side of the gap. Nine rings and she'd gone across every one of them. He smiled to see her safe. It quickly fell at the realisation he'd be making the journey soon.

A look down at the crowd and Flynn's eyes went to the Queen in amongst them. The huge red seat looked like a mobile throne and she relaxed in the luxury of it.

"Number two," Mistress called out. A smirk lifted her twisted face and she laughed as she said, "Jake Schwartz, how nice it is to see you again."

Like she'd done on the roof of the tall building, Mistress bullied Jake with her superior strength. A tight grip on the back of his shirt and she shoved him towards the edge of the roof like he was no more than a child. Flynn's heart raced to watch it and he listened to Jake whimper at what he must have assumed to be his end.

But Mistress stopped before she launched him off.

For the next few seconds, Jake cried and stared at his feet.

A look from him to the crowd, and Mistress said, "Come on now, Jakey-boy, I was only playing."

The crowd laughed, including the Queen, and Jake continued to sob.

Mistress stepped back from him while shaking her head. "You need to stop blubbering, Jake. Time to swing across, fella."

At least with Rose both going first and making it to the other side, it gave the others a blueprint to follow. As she had done, Jake sat down on the edge of the roof and dropped his legs over the side. The crowd clapped in time as he pulled the first ring up. They started slow, increasing in speed until he had a tight grip on the wooden circle.

Maybe the crowd couldn't see it, maybe they could, but from where he stood, Flynn saw the violent shake running through the man.

"Jake! Jake! Jake! Jake! Jake!" the crowd chanted and Flynn wanted to look away like he had with Rose. But he didn't. Instead, he watched Jake drop from the edge of the roof with a tight grip on the first ring.

As Jake swung through the air, the crowd cheered. He reached the end of the rope's long swing and Flynn muttered, "Let go." But Jake didn't.

A second too late and already on the back swing, Jake released his tight grip. He flew away from the next ring and dropped with a scream.

The crowd fell silent as he plummeted.

Chapter Thirty-Five

The entire cart shook with the impact of Jake's landing. A loud crash sounded out and the large wheels rocked back and forth before the crowd cheered.

When Flynn saw Jake impaled on the spikes below, his stomach lifted in a heave. He watched some of the crowd edge towards the cart. When they got close, a section of them threw their white slips of paper on him; most of which stuck to his bloody corpse.

The next few seconds lasted an age as Flynn stared at Jake's wide eyes. They showed a snapshot of his complete fear from falling. His mouth had been forced open by a stake that punctured through the back of his head. Blood glistened on what seemed to be the freshly sharpened stakes. It pooled on the flatbed of the trailer and ran off the sides of it.

Flynn looked at Mistress to see her stare down at the Queen.

When the Queen nodded, Mistress turned back to the line of prisoners yet to cross and called out, "Number four."

A young boy stepped forward. A teenager at best, he'd turned chalk white and Flynn saw the sun glisten off his sweating brow.

The kid looked less able than Jake had, but he surprised Flynn when he reached down and grabbed the first ring, slipping from the roof in one fluid movement. A gymnast, he moved from ring to ring as if he'd spent his entire life training for that moment.

At the end of each rope's swing, Flynn winced to watch him let go and catch the next ring along. Even the bloodthirsty crowd seemed to appreciate his effort, cheering while he moved across all nine rings as if he'd been born to do it. He jumped through the window frame on the other side to the applause of the crowd, Mistress, and even the Queen.

It took a few minutes for the noise to die down. When it finally had, Mistress turned to the brute. "Number seven, you're up."

As the thickset man walked to the edge of the roof, Flynn felt his heavy steps through the soles of his feet.

"Good luck following that," Mistress said to him.

A jaw that looked like it could crush rocks clenched tight enough to clamp through steel, and the brute looked at Mistress. He spoke from the side of his mouth in a low enough voice that Flynn heard it, but the crowd probably wouldn't have. "And what if I tell you to go fuck yourself?"

Flynn's heart galloped in anticipation of what would come next. Not that he gave a fuck about the brute, but an enraged Mistress would undoubtedly have an impact on his life.

As if mimicking the man, Mistress answered him with a similar low growl. Unlike the brute, her voice carried and the crowd clearly heard her. "Fuck with me and you get a ride off this roof on my boot. The choice is yours."

Everyone fell silent and Flynn glanced down at the Queen again. Hard not to look at her on her stupid throne as she stared up. She watched the drama unfold and pulled a strand of her straight black hair away from her face.

The brute and Mistress glared at one another before Mistress added, "Don't push me, fuck face."

Two gargantuan egos, the brute finally dropped his and sat down on the edge of the roof. Flynn watched his fine ginger hair dance in the breeze as he pulled the first ring to him. Many faces below stared up, their mouths open wide.

The brute's broad shoulders and large chest rose with a deep inhale and he slipped from the roof.

Nowhere near as graceful as the gymnast before him, the brute made it to the next ring. The physique of a primate, he clearly had the upper body strength and reach as he swung across, stretched out and grabbed the next ring. He repeated the process until he made it to the other side.

At the window, the brute reached out again, grabbed the frame, and dragged himself into the building. The crowd and the Queen showed their appreciation with their applause.

Mistress looked far from happy; her thin lips pressed tightly together, her jaw set. "Number nine," she said and a woman in her forties stepped forward. Maybe Flynn shouldn't write her off before she went, but she didn't look like she'd make it.

Nine swung forward on the first ring, reached out for the second one but lost her grip before she got to it. She spun through the air, cartwheeling for what felt like an eternity. The collective hiss of the crowd pulled a sharp breath in through their clenched teeth until the spikes halted her progress with a deep crunch. Silence and then a cheer from the crowd.

Nine lay over three spears. One ran through her neck, one her stomach, and one her thigh. Her long hair hung down and she bled out like Jake had. Fortunately, Flynn couldn't see her face from where he stood.

Eleven had already stepped forward by the time Flynn looked back up. She shook her head as she stared down at the carnage below. Mistress grinned at her, calmer than a moment ago. It looked like the death of nine had somehow relieved the fury she'd felt from her conversation with the brute. "Come on, love," she said to the woman.

Eleven continued to shake her head.

"Is that a no?"

Eleven nodded.

Mistress kicked her up the arse and sent her off the top of the roof with a scream. Another deep thud, silence, and then the crowd erupted into cheers and laughter.

The long black leather apron hung from Mistress as she bowed to the crowd. She then turned and smiled at Flynn.

Flynn's legs shook to be the focus of Mistress' attention. "Come on," the vicious woman hissed. "It's your turn now, handsome."

A gulp did nothing for Flynn's dry throat, and when he looked down at the crowd, he felt every pair of eyes on him. After pulling in a deep breath, Flynn stepped forward to the edge of the roof, sat down and hung his legs over. He pulled the first ring up, looked at the dead prisoners on the medieval carts, looked at the Queen and her icy glare, and grabbed the ring in a tight grip.

"Come on, sweetie," Mistress said, "we don't have all fucking day."

Chapter Thirty-Six

Flynn should have done more than sit on the edge of the roof and look at the people down below.

He should have done more than stare at the wooden stakes with the bodies of the fallen prisoners pinned to them.

He should have avoided the hypnotic lure of the dripping blood as it plopped from the sides of each trailer and disappeared beneath the press of the spectators' feet.

It made no sense to look at the Queen, to get dragged into her dark stare.

But Flynn did all of those things.

Flynn's body locked tight, tense with inaction. He continued to sit on the edge of the roof, his head spinning and his stomach turning until Mistress cleared her throat at him.

The dark stare of the broad woman bored into Flynn and she didn't need to tell him he'd best move soon or else.

A look across at the building opposite and Flynn saw Rose stare back at him. Unlike the crowd below, she didn't jeer or goad him. As if knowing exactly what he needed, she made a fist with her right hand and pumped it twice against her chest. It showed him she believed in him. Someone had to.

Flynn entered a moment of weightlessness as he slipped from the roof. It ended abruptly when the rope snapped taut.

Any healing Flynn's brand had gone through got ripped open when his legs swung beneath him as he moved forward. He wanted to scream at the pain over his right kidney. Instead, he clenched his teeth and rode out the agony while heading towards the next ring.

The summer heat had turned Flynn's palms damp, and as he reached the end of the first rope's swing, his hand slipped, propelling him towards the second ring.

Another moment of weightlessness, this time with no guaranteed resistance of the rope saving him.

The crowd below gasped as Flynn grabbed the next ring.

Flynn's arms burned with the effort of the swing, his momentum carrying him forward. He caught the next ring slightly more easily than the last. Maybe he could do this.

Just before he jumped again, a projectile came from the crowd and crashed into Flynn's right eye. A white flash of light exploded through his vision and his world blurred in front of him. Blinded, he couldn't make the next jump.

As Flynn swung backwards, away from his destination, he saw the chaos below, even with blurred vision. What must have been the person to throw the missile at him—be it a rock, or fruit, or whatever the fuck they'd thrown—had already been dragged from the crowd by women dressed in royal blue. They must have been the Queen's guards.

A sharp sting sat in Flynn's right eye and he blinked repeatedly to try to ease the pain of it as he watched events unfold below. The royal blue guards dragged the woman to the side and lay into her with a flurry of kicks.

Each swing moved a shorter distance than the one before it and Flynn eventually came to a complete halt. He reached up and held the ring above him with both hands. He stared down at the crowd and the crowd stared back. Open mouths, wide eyes, pale faces. They looked nervous. They should try being in his position.

Flynn looked away from the woman taking the beating and put his attention on Rose again. She stared back at him and pushed her clenched fists out in front of her. She pulled them back and then pushed them forward in a rocking motion and Flynn nodded at her. It would be the only way.

First Flynn pulled his legs back and then swung them forwards. He did it several times to no effect. The ring above him moved, but he couldn't get any swinging action going.

A look down at the stakes on the trailer beneath him and Flynn saw the woman who had cartwheeled through the air before impaling herself on them. Sweat ran into his eyes from the heat and his effort. His heart raced. When he looked at Rose again, he shook his head. He couldn't do it.

This time Rose used her hands to press down on the air in front of her. She mouthed, *slow it down!*

Another deep breath and Flynn tried to follow her advice. He pulled his legs back and let the ring shift a few inches with him. He then rocked forwards. He went with the movement of the ring as he swayed forwards and then backwards, forwards and then backwards.

It worked! Slowly but surely, Flynn's momentum picked up

and he got the ring swinging again. The crowd below cheered when he looked down. They were all getting behind his efforts. The woman who threw the projectile at him now lay either dead or unconscious on the ground, ignored by everyone.

Flynn got to the rope's maximum swing. He did several more before he trusted he couldn't get it to swing any farther and then he let go.

Unlike on his other attempts, this time Flynn flew forwards with both hands out in front of him rather than just one. His stomach lifted as he rose through the air, and seemed to sink a few seconds after his body did as he came back down again.

The snap of his body weight against the ring ran down Flynn's arms and into his shoulders. He clenched his teeth against the pain of it. The brand on his back ripped open again and he could almost hear it smack its tacky lips as the scabs tore.

But he held on. Of course he fucking held on. Whatever strength he needed, he had it. Anything to avoid those damn spikes.

A different method to those who went before him, Flynn repeated what had just worked for him. He got the fifth ring swinging as far as it could and let go again. He did the same with the sixth, the seventh, the eighth.

One left between Flynn and the building on the other side. Rose remained in the window, staring at him and silently willing him on.

Flynn got the eighth ring swinging as far as it would go before he jumped for the ninth. The crowd below went wild as he flew through the air and caught it. A look down as he swung and he saw even the Queen grinned at his acrobatics. Maybe he'd made a new fan.

When Flynn had the final ring at its maximum swing, he let go and leapt for the empty window frame where Rose waited for him.

At that moment, the brute walked across the space he headed for and bent over as if to tie his shoelace. He showed Flynn his arse and completely blocked off his access to the derelict building.

As Flynn flew through the air, staring at the large man's rear end, his resolve faltered and his muscles turned slack. He had no way through.

Chapter Thirty-Seven

If Rose hadn't pulled the brute's T-shirt and tugged him away, Flynn wouldn't have made it through the window.

The large ginger man—already leaning forward—crashed down on his crown against the hard floor with a loud *thunk* that echoed through the empty building. From the way Rose bit down on her bottom lip, she clearly dragged him with all the force she had.

Flynn sailed over the top of the brute and fell into the abandoned space. Before he had a chance to get to his feet, the brute had jumped up and had Rose pinned against the wall. Blood ran from the fresh cut on his forehead as he screamed in her face, "What the fuck? Are you trying to start something?"

Exhausted from the past few days, Flynn pushed through it, jumped up, and shoulder barged the brute. It sent him stumbling as Flynn shouted, "Get off her!"

The large ginger meathead turned on Flynn and lifted a fist, ready to punch him.

Flynn raised his guard, but the blow never landed.

When Flynn lowered his hands, he saw several guards pull

the man back and pin him to the ground. It took the weight of three fully grown men to keep him down. Even then, he shook and twisted beneath their pressure and it looked like he might buck them off.

It took for Mistress to call through the room to silence the scuffle. "At ease, you fat fuck." She walked over to the brute, hands on her hips as she stared down at him. "You try anything like that again and you're getting launched onto those spikes out there. You understand?"

The brute didn't reply, so Mistress leaned in towards him, their noses close to touching. "You understand?"

A wince twisted his red face as if it caused him pain to back down. He finally nodded his compliance.

"Good," she said, pulled a black hood from her back pocket, and slipped it over his head.

Before Flynn had a chance to think, a hood covered his head too. Rough hands then pulled his arms behind his back.

Chapter Thirty-Eight

The hood was ripped so quickly from Flynn's head, the rough fabric of it made the end of his nose sting. He rubbed it as he walked to try to ease the slight buzzing pain.

Not that Flynn focused on the sensation for long. Not with what he saw in front of him. A box of a structure about five metres square, it stood about one metre from the ground. It had been completely covered in both black sheets and blue tarpaulins. It looked like they'd run out of one while trying to cover the structure, so they finished it off with the other. At the front he could see an entranceway of sorts. A crawlspace.

Because he hadn't had the hood on for long, the sun stung Flynn's eyes, but it didn't blind him. Now rubbing his eyes rather than his nose, he looked at the crowd gathered around the strange structure.

Abandoned buildings ran down either side of the old high street. The crawlspace looked to be in what Vicky had referred to previously as a pedestrian area. She would always laugh when she said that. Everywhere was a pedestrian area now.

A look to either side and Flynn saw Rose on his left and the three other prisoners on his right. The brute, the teenage boy, and a slim woman who'd waited behind him at the rings. A man had also waited, but he couldn't see him.

All four of them looked fitter than the brute, and maybe the sheen of sweat on his red face had more to do with his fear than the summer heat.

"Okay," Mistress called out as she stepped in front of the prisoners. "Just two people will make it through this event. This game is called the rat run. A crawl-through maze, it only has one entrance and one exit. The first two to come out of the other side win. The rest …" She giggled and glanced at the guards behind her. Six of them in total, they all carried a bloodstained sledgehammer each.

"You!" Mistress said and pointed at the brute. "You have a one-minute penalty because of your behaviour earlier."

The brute's face fell slack.

"I let you get away with killing someone on shit hill, but now you've tried it again, you need to pay the price. These games may be brutal, but they have rules."

"But they'll be out the other side of that thing in one minute," the brute said. "I won't have a chance."

The same twisted grin turned Mistress' face into a leer and she said, "Two minutes."

"What the fuck?"

"Three minutes."

Murmurs came from the crowd at that moment and a large section of them dropped their small slips of paper. They must have had number seven on them.

The brute's already red face turned redder and he opened his mouth to respond, but Mistress cut him off. "Try me," she said. "You're lucky I'm even giving you a chance with the way you've carried on."

A heavy sigh and the brute slumped where he stood. He then looked at the guards behind him, who closed in while gripping their sledgehammers.

At least Flynn wouldn't be in the maze with him. His underhanded tactics would undoubtedly come into play when the guards couldn't see him. A glance at the other two prisoners and he drew a deep breath. They seemed straight up, but who knew what they'd do. They were all fighting for their lives. Hell, even Rose could turn on him.

"If you're wondering," Mistress said to the others as she paced up and down in front of them, her leather apron flapping with her movement, "Twenty didn't make it. He resisted a little bit too much and got a ride on my boot from the roof." She looked at the prisoners as if daring one of them to say something. None of them replied.

"Right!" Mistress yelled and Flynn jumped at her loud call. A shake ran through him as he looked from Mistress to the guards to the sledgehammers in their grips, and finally to the maze.

"All except you"—Mistress pointed at the brute—"line up in number order. Like I said, the first two out of the rat run will be allowed to take the final jump to safety. The others …" She looked at each prisoner in turn, and by the time she got to Flynn at the back of the queue, she laughed. "Well, it was nice knowing you. You fought well."

A couple of people in the crowd laughed, although when

Flynn looked at them, he saw sombre expressions. Almost as if they'd gotten to know the prisoners and cared about their fate at that point. Their reactions also spoke of what would come to the ones who didn't make it. He looked at the guards and their sledgehammers again.

"Number one," Mistress called to Rose, who stepped forward. While pointing at the small tunnel entrance to the rat run, she said, "Go!"

Rose dropped down onto her knees and disappeared into the darkness.

"Number four." The teenage boy followed behind.

"Number sixteen."

As Flynn crawled into the small maze, he listened to Mistress say, "And last, but certainly not least, number eighteen. Good luck."

Chapter Thirty-Nine

The hard concrete ground burned Flynn's kneecaps and he felt grazes opening up instantly. Not that he could do anything about it.

The maze had been so completely covered, the only light in the place came from the entrance behind them. The air in the hot space stank of sweat. It left a flat taste on his dry tongue.

When Flynn crashed face first into a wall in front of him, his world rocked from the blow as if it had been tilted on its axis. A solid wooden barrier, he couldn't afford to crash into any more of them and still remain conscious. A shake of his head cleared it a little.

The scuffling sound of the other prisoners ran away from Flynn in different directions. Fuck knew where they went, the twisting maze offering too many choices already.

When a hand grabbed Flynn, he turned in the direction of it and raised his fist.

But then she spoke. "Flynn?"

"Rose? Do you know the way out of here?"

Rose took his hand and guided it over to the wall next to them. A groove ran through it.

"What is it?" Flynn asked.

"The way out of here. Feel it," Rose said, "it's been carved into the wall on purpose. The way it runs up and down, I dunno, it seems to be here for our help."

"What if it's a trick?"

"What other options do we have?"

The second Flynn took to think about it already felt like too long. All the while they debated what to do, the other two were getting closer to the exit. "Come on, then," Flynn said. "Let's follow it."

Rose led the way and, although too dark for him to see her, Flynn heard her ahead of him as he followed the trail along the wooden wall with his right hand.

Every shuffle forwards seemed to take more skin from Flynn's kneecaps. The hard ground became sandpaper against his fragile body. His trousers did little to protect his knees. Not that a few grazes mattered compared to the sledgehammers waiting for third place and below.

Within about ten seconds, Flynn's clothes clung to his sweating form. But he pushed on, the hot air hard to breathe, his throat close to cracking with dryness.

***

Several twists and turns later and Flynn saw daylight up ahead. "We've *found* it, Rose."

But Rose didn't respond. Instead, she sped up as she headed for what looked to be the maze's exit, the scuffle of her knees and shoes scratching over the hard ground.

But what if they'd gone full circle? What if they were about to step out of the entrance to the maze rather than the exit? Not that they had any other choice. They had to check it out.

Rose slipped from the maze first and Flynn crawled out a second later, back into the glare of the sun. When he stood up, the slight breeze cooled him and he looked over the top of the maze to see the brute on the other side, waiting by the entrance. He hadn't even had the chance to enter it.

Chapter Forty

"Great!" the large ginger man called out, his arms falling limp at his sides. But before he could say anything else, a guard next to him bit down on his bottom lip and swung his sledgehammer.

The loud *crack* ran a weakness through Flynn's legs that nearly threw him to the ground. He watched the hammer catch the brute flush on the temple, robbing him of his next complaint, turning his legs bandy, and knocking him down dead.

"Well done," Mistress squealed and walked over to Flynn and Rose as if a man hadn't just been executed right behind them. A broad grin split her witch's face. "You found the trail, didn't you?"

Neither Flynn nor Rose replied, both of them looking between Mistress and the dead brute on the other side of the maze.

"Oh, look," Mistress said and hunched down to peer into the maze's exit. She sang the next few words as if in celebration of what would come. "Here comes another one."

One of the guards with a sledgehammer ran over and wound it back.

When the woman in her mid-twenties poked her head from the maze, the guard swung for her and yelled, "Fore!"

Flynn winced and turned away to the sound of the crowd laughing and a deep crunch as the woman's skull gave in. When he looked back, two more guards each had an arm of the woman and were dragging her limp form from the maze. Blood ran from the huge dent in the side of her head.

They dragged the dead woman past Mistress, who paid her no attention. The life of a number didn't matter.

Nobody spoke as the scuffling sound of the final prisoner called out of the maze. Flynn's ragged breaths rocked his tired frame and every time he swallowed, a heave lifted up his throat from the dryness turning it tacky.

As the sound of the teenager grew louder, Flynn's pulse sped up. He'd be sticking his head from the maze any time soon and some oaf with a sledgehammer would try to knock it clean off his shoulders.

Flynn saw Mistress nod at the next sledgehammer guard, who ran to the maze's exit and wound his weapon back like the other one had.

It took just a few more seconds before the prisoner poked his head from the maze. He didn't seem to notice the guard, because he looked up at Mistress and smiled. The poor bastard thought he'd won.

The sledgehammer clattered into the side of his face, forcing his left eye out and turning him instantly flaccid. The blow opened a deep split in the boy's head and Flynn turned his back on him. He'd seen enough.

Chapter Forty-One

Flynn kept his back turned on the dead prisoner at the maze's exit. The sound of dragging feet ran over the ground from where some of the guards pulled the corpse away, but he still didn't look back. It took for someone to tap him on the shoulder before he turned around.

Where he'd expected to see Mistress, he gasped to see the Queen staring at him.

Flynn glanced at Rose, who watched on with her mouth wide. He then looked back at the Queen and her angular features.

After several dry gulps, Flynn accepted he wouldn't get his breath back and did his best to ride out his fear. He tried to speak in the presence of her stony expression, opening and closing his mouth several times. But he couldn't find the words.

A stiff back that ran all the way up to an arched eyebrow and the Queen spoke. "Quite squeamish, it would seem."

He didn't reply.

A look from Flynn to Rose and back to Flynn again and she said, "You two came out of there awfully close together. One might think you were working as a team."

"Um …" Flynn said.

Before he could say anything else, the Queen spoke again. "It's fine. Work together all you like. You're not trying to kill each other"—she glanced over at where the brute had been—"like lesser people would do. I admire that."

When Flynn followed her line of sight, he saw they'd taken the brute away and were dragging him into an abandoned shop. The other two prisoners were being taken that way too.

"It's how we get to use this town for our games," the Queen said.

Flynn stared at her.

"We don't live here. This town, like most towns in the area, are hostile places run by gangs. We use it for holding our prisoners and for the games. In return, they get eighteen fresh corpses as payment every time."

Another look at the shop the bodies had been dragged into and Flynn looked for the rats in the shadows. He didn't see any.

"Despite their brutish appearance," the Queen said, "the gang who run this town are quite nice when you get to know them. And no one in my community eats people. There isn't any point when you can trap animals."

The thud of Flynn's heart boomed through him. He'd finally recovered his breath, but he currently existed on the edge of a panic attack. If he said or did the wrong thing, the gang would have nineteen corpses to feed on.

Flynn straightened his back as if it would help compose him, and although he stood taller than the Queen, her presence dwarfed him.

"Anyway," the Queen said, "One and Sixteen, only one of

you can walk away from this. We need to take you to the final trial of this course. The winner will be welcomed into our community. The loser will be trapped and imprisoned again. They'll get their chance to escape, but they'll have to go through the games again to do it."

A glance at Rose and Flynn saw her pale hue. No doubt he looked as bad. Neither of them wanted to go back to that prison. But could he sell her out to save himself?

"Come on, darlings," the Queen said as she walked away, her hips swaying, her dark trousers clinging to her tight bottom. "Follow me."

Chapter Forty-Two

They used the back of an old lorry. It had been patched up after years of corrosion had taken bites from it. A completely new wooden top lay across it. Hopefully the rusty frame could support their weight.

Two ladders rested against the lorry.

"You have to pick one each," the Queen said. "One, you go first."

Before she went to her ladder, Rose walked over to Flynn and lifted his left hand with hers. Not a shake, more a gentle squeeze. "Good luck," she muttered and pulled a tight smile at him.

The breath left Flynn's lungs as he stared at the girl. Only one of them would walk away from this. If only they'd met in better circumstances. Because he didn't have the words, he simply nodded at her.

Rose dropped Flynn's hand and picked the left ladder. Flynn walked over to the right.

As the pair climbed to the top, the crowd fell silent, many of them watching on with open mouths. Even the Queen seemed gripped by what she saw, her attention on Rose more than Flynn. His pulse quickened, anxiety buzzing in his guts. She'd made the correct choice, he knew it. He'd have to go through the games again.

When they reached the wooden roof of the old trailer, the Queen called out to them. "Now wait, I need to get around to the other side."

In the time it took the Queen to walk around the trailer, Flynn looked down at where they had to jump. Two piles of soiled mattresses.

The Queen said, "One pile will give way and throw you back into prison." She winked up at Rose. "One of you will have to start all over again and earn the number one brand."

It suddenly dawned on Flynn and he looked from Rose to the Queen and back to Rose again. "This is your *second* time around."

Why hadn't he seen it before? Rose's number one brand had been over her left kidney where everyone else had them over their right.

Rose winced as if apologising and lifted her shirt to reveal the skin over her right kidney. It had an angry red cross branded through the number six. "I'm sorry, Flynn."

"So you knew which ladder to pick? You bitch."

Rose shook her head. "I'm sorry."

"Right!" the Queen called out before Flynn could say anything else. "On my count, I want you both to jump. The best of luck to you. May the best person win. Although I think we all know who'll win this one."

"One," the Queen called and Flynn ground his jaw. He'd have to go through the games again.

"Two."

Although Flynn stared at Rose, she didn't look back at him. Tears ran down her cheeks and she shook where she stood. "I can't believe you've screwed me over," he said to her.

"Three."

For a brief moment neither of them jumped. The Queen stared up at them and said, "Don't make me say it again."

"Fuck you, Rose," Flynn said and he jumped. He saw Rose in his peripheral vision jump with him.

Chapter Forty-Three

As Flynn crashed down, he flinched in anticipation of the mattresses giving way beneath him. When they didn't, the shock of it snapped up his body from the ground remaining firm.

The pile of mattresses beside him folded in on themselves and pulled Rose under.

Flynn stared at the hole Rose had vanished through and the crowd erupted into cheers and whoops. Because the mattresses had fallen down the hole with her, they'd covered her, obscuring her from his view.

When Flynn looked at the Queen, he saw her smiling. "What just happened?"

A tilt of her head to one side and she said, "You won, my dear."

"Did you switch the holes around? Did you trick Rose?"

"No. Number one knew exactly what she was doing."

Flynn's jaw dropped and he lost his breath for a second. "She *knew* she'd picked the route back to the prison?"

The Queen's smile broadened and she spoke loud enough for everyone to hear. "She did. What a gesture, eh?"

Some of the crowd made soft sounds at Rose's sacrifice.

"It would seem she values *your* freedom more than her own, Flynn. Notice how you're Flynn now too? You're not a number anymore. You've made it, honey."

The way she called him *honey* sent a chill snaking through Flynn. But his mind quickly returned to Rose and he looked into the hole next to him again. She lay beneath the pile of mattresses somewhere, waiting to be taken back to the prison. Why had she sacrificed herself for him?

Before Flynn could say anything else, a couple of the Queen's guards came forward. Two women dressed in royal blue, one of them had a sack in her hands.

"Please forgive the need to cover your face again," the Queen said, "but we still want to keep the whereabouts of our community secret. We don't know if we can trust you yet."

The world turned dark as one of the guards slipped the hood over Flynn's head. It had a halitosis reek from having been used a lot, and he screwed his nose up against the stale smell of it.

"We're going to take you back, feed you, clothe you, and let you get some rest. No one will ever talk about you being in the games again. Once you enter our community, the shame of the trials is left behind. But know this, you've just earned the respect of everyone in the royal complex. It's no mean feat getting through the games. Well done, Flynn, you've proven yourself worthy." She raised her voice. "Let's hear it for the champ!"

The crowd erupted. The white noise of it beneath the hood spun Flynn out more than before.

Much more gentle than the previous guards, the royal guards led Flynn away. Whatever happened, he needed to get Rose out of that dungeon. He owed her everything.

Chapter Forty-Four

If Flynn were to guess, he'd say about half an hour had passed. In that time, he'd walked a little way and then rode on the back of a cart, which, from the clop, clop, clopping noise, he assumed to be pulled by a horse or donkey.

He heard huge gates open. They passed through them and finally the cart stopped. Someone helped him down, gentle in their handling of him. It stood in stark contrast to how they'd treated him in the dungeon and he didn't trust it one bit. Because he'd seen just how cruel this community could be, he refused to lower his guard.

Flynn walked over uneven ground—it felt like it might be a field—then it levelled out and the acoustics changed, the snap of their footsteps showing they'd entered a building of some sort.

Although Flynn had plenty of questions, he didn't ask any. They'd called him the victor, but he'd been a prisoner until then. A prisoner who had no right to ask anything. The illusion of free will didn't wash with him, especially with the hood still over his head.

It sounded like the space they walked through opened up. The echo off the walls and ceiling showed it stretched wide and high. The sound of footsteps that had been behind him pulled next to him as their party clearly spread out. A group of people with him, but he couldn't begin to guess at how many. If he tried to fight now, he'd undoubtedly lose.

Besides, Flynn needed to save Rose. He needed to bide his time and work out where they kept her so he could get her out. As wary as it made him to be there, he had no other choice. Anywhere else and he wouldn't have a chance of finding her location.

The acoustics changed again as they entered what sounded like another corridor. The walls and ceiling sounded like they'd closed in and just one pair of footsteps came with him.

Then they stopped. The person with him snapped what sounded like a door handle down and the gentle creak of hinges called out through the quiet. They grabbed Flynn's elbow and gently led him into the space before pulling his hood away.

Every time they'd removed Flynn's hood, he'd had to blink against the change in light. Now they'd done it inside, the adjustment felt much less violent.

When he could see, Flynn took the place in. A room larger than the one he'd had in Home, it had a window too. It had a double bed in the middle of it and a chair in one corner, suggesting he might actually get some leisure time in this place. A tin bath lay beneath the window with a bucket of water beside it.

He'd been so busy taking in the room, he only now noticed who'd led him in there. A step back as he looked at her regal face and he stammered, "Um … I'm sorry, I didn't realise it was you. Sorry."

The Queen smiled at him. A genuine smile for the first time since he'd seen her watching the games. She seemed much more relaxed than before. Her look spoke of a friend much more than a leader as she said, "Welcome to the royal complex."

Before Flynn could reply, she added, "There are some clothes on the bed for you. Get yourself cleaned up and I'll show you the rest of the place when you're done." And with that, she left him alone in the room.

Chapter Forty-Five

The clean joggers lay soft against Flynn's freshly washed skin. A bit too thick for the summer heat, but it felt great to wear something comfortable and clean. Especially when the bath water had been so cold.

Despite warming up since he'd dried off, Flynn still felt the shock of the frigid bath in his tense muscles. The brand on his back burned from being submerged and no doubt had infection deep inside of it.

Flynn stared at the door to his room as he walked towards it. It had a small round window in it for people to look in, but he couldn't see anything outside other than the wall opposite.

When he stepped out, Flynn found the Queen waiting in the corridor like she said she would. "Sorry to keep you," he said.

She pulled her straight black hair behind her left ear and shook her head. "Don't be sorry, you needed to get yourself cleaned up." She looked him up and down. "How's the brand?"

Like she gave a fuck. "Sore."

"I can imagine. We have a cream for that. I'll make sure you get some."

It would have been nice if the cunt hadn't branded him in the first place. Despite her niceties now, he couldn't forget what she did to people. The kind of sick freak who made murder a sport. He couldn't ever forget that.

Another broad smile at Flynn, her teeth whiter than any should be in this new world, and the Queen turned around and walked off. He followed her, taking the place in by looking around where he hadn't been able to before.

The corridor with his room on it had many similar rooms running along either side. Much like Home, but without the dingy underground feel to it.

"So what is this place?" Flynn asked.

The Queen laughed and shook her head. "You're so young."

Flynn didn't reply.

"It used to be a hospital. That would be obvious if you were slightly older. I suppose you probably never visited one of these."

"I did when I was two and broke my arm. But that was a long time ago and I can't remember it."

They walked the rest of the way in silence. The Queen kept the pace quick, her black leather boots slamming down against the hard floor.

Despite being repulsed by the woman, Flynn found himself staring at her arse in her tight black trousers. Every time he tried to look up, his eyes soon dropped down to it again.

Chapter Forty-Six

What must have been the hospital's foyer opened up at the end of the corridor. Rows and rows of chairs were covered in dust from disuse. Many of them had ripped cushions, the foam padding from inside lolling out of them like yellowed tongues.

The Queen walked straight through the area and Flynn followed her. As they moved, he looked at the dead monitors on the walls. They must have been useful in the old world. Now they collected dust, much like the ones in Home's canteen.

A small corridor led to a large set of double doors that had been wedged open. Flynn followed the Queen out of them into the bright sunlight, where he looked at the larger complex.

A huge fence ran around the outside of the place. Entire trees had been stripped and stacked next to one another much like they'd done at Home. The fence stood about four or five metres tall and looked like it could withstand anything people could throw at it.

Most of the space in front of the hospital had been turned into farmland and Flynn saw maybe twenty people working the fields.

"We only sleep in the hospital," the Queen said as she watched Flynn take the place in. She pointed over at a large wooden barn. "We use that place to eat in and get together as a community." A ruffle of her nose and she screwed her face up as if she had a bitter taste in her mouth. "Something about hospitals gives me the chills. Ghastly places really."

Flynn didn't comment. Too young to have a decent memory of them, he hadn't had a chance to associate them with anything yet. Although that would undoubtedly change.

"People have different roles in the royal complex," the Queen said. "You're either a hunter, a cleaner, or a farmer. You can request to be one of them, but ultimately I decide where we need you most. And if I can offer you a little advice, I'd say you should set your heart on being a hunter." She ran her eyes up and down his body, the tip of her tongue poking through her thin lips as she did it. "You're such a strapping lad, I wouldn't want to waste what you have."

Heat rushed to Flynn's cheeks and he looked down at the ground. She'd eat him alive given half a chance.

"Come on," the Queen said and smacked him on the arse. "We're in time for lunch, and everyone's waiting to meet you."

Once she'd pulled a few steps ahead of him, Flynn's gaze returned to her athletic form.

Chapter Forty-Seven

The closer Flynn walked to the large barn, the louder the chatter spilling out of it. There were clearly a lot of people inside. The Queen stopped ahead of him, and when he caught up to her, she forced her arm through his, linking them like a father of the bride would with his daughter. She then led them towards the barn's wide-open front doors.

As they drew nearer, Flynn saw more and more people in the barn, although they hadn't seen him yet. It took for him and the Queen to enter the hot space before everyone fell silent and looked over.

The tight pack of bodies and lack of ventilation added to Flynn's nerves and he started to sweat. A hot summer day made hotter by being crammed inside. Many of the staring faces glistened with perspiration too. No doubt the barn would be great in the winter, but it felt like too much that day.

Where Flynn had expected the people in the room to throw themselves prostrate at their Queen's entrance, they didn't. Reverence for their leader, sure, but not blind subservience. Maybe she ruled with respect rather than fear. Although, none of that mattered because he'd experienced what the vicious cunt did to her prisoners. He'd never have anything but resentment for the horrible bitch.

"Ladies and gentlemen, boys and girls, I'd like to introduce you to your new champion." She turned to Flynn and said, "Flynn …" She then paused, leaned close to him, and spoke so only he could hear. "What's your surname?"

Flynn replied with similar hushed tones. "Golding."

A cocked eyebrow and the Queen said to him, "One of life's winners, it would seem." She then turned to the room and announced, "Flynn Golding!"

Most of the room got to their feet and clapped. A group of people at a large table laden with food banged their metal cups against the wooden surface but didn't stand up. Flynn looked across at them and then back at the Queen. "They had number sixteen," she said. "Today they're royalty."

Now fully in the barn, Flynn inhaled the smell of cooked meat. Although the canteen at Home had an essence of meat in their broths, they mostly ate vegetarian. The rich smell made his stomach rumble.

A long table sat at the head of the room with two empty spaces at it. The large chair in the middle was vacant. A grand throne, it had a high back and red cushioning. The seat next to it also sat empty. The perfect space for a little man toy. A look down at their still-linked arms and Flynn sighed.

On either side of the empty seats sat a row of women. All of them wore royal blue. All of them—his stomach sank—except one. The broad-shouldered, hook-nosed, vicious witch looked at him and smiled. It turned his blood cold.

When the Queen headed in the direction of the table, she dragged Flynn over with her.

Although Mistress looked at Flynn, he didn't look back. Regardless of how she wanted to play it now, he wouldn't forgive what she'd done. He couldn't. To forgive anyone in this community would make him one of them, and that wouldn't happen. Mistress would pay for branding him like a cow.

The community might have welcomed Flynn in, but he didn't belong there. As hospitable as they were, he couldn't ever forget what they did to people.

Once they'd sat down, Flynn looked over the sea of staring faces. Seeing one hundred and fifty people or more, he leaned closed to the Queen. "Is this everyone in the community?"

The Queen nodded. "Meal times are important. Wherever possible, we all eat together."

"Even the guards on the gates?"

A cold stare came back at Flynn. "People in this area don't fuck with this community. Even if they did manage to get past the massive wall, they wouldn't last two minutes once inside."

An arm came over Flynn's right shoulder and placed a plate in front of him. It had a cooked bird on it that looked like a pigeon, although it smelled great. A smile at the woman who'd delivered his food and he turned to his host.

The Queen nodded down at his plate. "You'll be surprised just how good those flying rats taste."

Several bowls lined the table in front of Flynn. Roasted potatoes and salads, he reached across and took a generous helping of each. His stomach continued to rumble as he filled his plate.

Once he'd loaded up on food, Flynn looked to see no one else had started yet. He leaned back in his chair to wait, but winced at the electric pain of his brand against the back of his wooden seat. A glance at Mistress and he found her staring straight back at him. She'd pay for what she did to him.

When Flynn looked back at the Queen, he saw her assessing him with her cold blue eyes. "I'm so sorry," she said, even though she didn't look it. She clicked her fingers and looked for someone to answer her call.

A boy of about twelve years old ran over and dipped his head to his leader. The Queen pointed at Flynn. "Get him some cream for his brand, would you?"

The boy nodded again and ran off. Flynn shared another look with Mistress.

Still no one ate, so Flynn held back too, his hunger gnawing away at both his stomach and patience.

At that moment, the Queen tapped her knife against her metal cup and stood up. The hall fell silent, every sweating face turning their way.

It had been intimidating to walk into the place, but now Flynn sat at the head of the room, it felt even worse. Every face stared his way. Easily as large as Home's canteen, the vast space didn't look like it could hold any more people.

Easier to admire the structure instead of looking at the crowd, Flynn looked up at the bare wooden ceiling. Beams as wide as tree trunks ran through it. As well as the smell of cooked meats, Flynn also caught the whiff of the exposed wood.

"Now," the Queen said, pulling Flynn's attention back down to the room, "before we eat, I want to officially welcome

Flynn Golding to this community. The games have proven he's earned a spot here. He's been through the toughest challenges and come out the other side. After today, we don't mention the games to him. He's not a former prisoner anymore, he's one of us."

A pain twisted through Flynn's chest to think of how Rose let him win. To think of her in that horrible dungeon again.

"Resources are in short supply in this self-sufficient world, but when we find someone who meets our challenges, what do we do?"

The call came back from the room as a loud boom and Flynn flinched when the sound smashed into him. "WE MAKE SPACE!"

A broad smile and the Queen nodded. "We do, we make space. So you have a new brother now. Treat him as you would expect to be treated and this society will continue to be great." She lowered her voice. "And it will continue to work out for you."

The threat sent a shimmer around the room. They knew who ran this place and they all danced to the beat of her drum. Despite her smile, Flynn now saw she clearly ruled the community with zero tolerance. The facade he'd seen when first entering the barn had already been shattered.

Nods and grunts of approval swept around the barn. Just like that, Flynn had become one of them. As the Queen sat down again, Flynn focused on his food. Nothing else mattered at that moment.

Chapter Forty-Eight

Flynn kept his head down for most of the meal. The Queen had been right about the pigeon; it tasted amazing.

Mistress continued to sit three people away from Flynn on his right, but he didn't look at her anymore. He didn't want to be put off his meal and he had nothing to say to the bitch. Although he felt her look across at him several times in his peripheral vision, he ignored her attention.

Towards the end of the meal, the boy the Queen had called over tapped Flynn on the shoulder and handed him some cream.

Flynn looked at the old tube.

"Nappy rash cream," the Queen said.

Flynn looked at her.

"It works wonders with wounds."

He had no reason to doubt it. After all, what harm could it do. A shrug and Flynn put the tube in his pocket for later.

Chapter Forty-Nine

Most people had finished the meal when the Queen banged her metal goblet against the table.

The place fell silent.

"Time for the entertainment," she announced. The stern look on her face sank dread through Flynn as the mood in the place twisted another notch darker.

The people were clearly used to the routine because they didn't need any further instructions. As one, they all stood up and moved the tables to the sides of the barn.

Flynn and those at the top table remained seated.

By the time the people had cleared a large space in the middle, two guards walked in with what appeared to be a prisoner each. One man and one woman, fortunately not Rose. Everyone watched the entrance.

The Queen stood up, her tone as sombre as her glare. "You all know Jason."

No one spoke as the male prisoner dropped his head to stare at the ground.

"I allowed him the presence of my company on *many*

occasions. I trusted him and gave him one of the highest positions in this community."

At that moment, Flynn felt a lot of the people in the room look at him.

Jason looked to be about Flynn's age. Twenty-five, maybe thirty. A good ten years younger than the Queen at least.

"But he *violated* my trust," the Queen said, her hand shaking as she pulled her long black hair behind her right ear. "He fell in love."

The female prisoner, a young and beautiful woman barely in her twenties, shook and cried, flinching away from the Queen's accusation.

"Now they must both pay."

Flynn's full stomach clamped around his undigested meal as he watched Jason and his love get dragged into the middle of the cleared space. Both of them stared down, awaiting what would undoubtedly be a brutal punishment.

Although Flynn didn't look at Mistress, he noticed her nod in his peripheral vision in response to the Queen signalling at her. She got to her feet, walked around the table, and up to the prisoners in the middle of the barn.

Mistress' leather apron flapped with every step she took forward. She drew a knife from her belt while she walked. A scimitar, it caught the dull light in the room and sparkled. If a weapon could grin, the shiny curved blade carried mirth up to Jason and his love.

Near silence fell on the room as Mistress approached Jason first. She raised the sharp tip of her blade to his eye. She then rested the short sword against his throat. Flynn saw Jason gulp at the applied pressure.

But Mistress stopped there. Instead of cutting him, she said, "Strip."

Jason froze, but when Mistress said, "Don't make me ask again," he slowly peeled his clothes off.

Mistress looked at the woman next to Jason. "And you, princess."

The woman shook worse than ever, but she took her clothes off all the same, sobbing as she did it.

Despite the tense atmosphere balling nausea in Flynn's guts, he couldn't look away from the beautiful young woman as she got naked. No wonder Jason had been tempted by her.

When the two prisoners were done, the Queen got to her feet. "Now, I wouldn't want anyone to say I'm not fair. I don't mind people falling in love, that happens. But, Jason, sweetie, you *betrayed* me. She looked down at his flaccid cock and raised an eyebrow. "Just couldn't keep it in your trousers, could you?"

Some of the crowd laughed, but nowhere near as much as the female guards beside the Queen and Flynn.

At that moment, another guard walked in with a chicken. The stupid creature twisted and tried to flap its wings, but the guard had a tight grip on it.

"The first one to catch the chicken," the Queen said, "gets to avoid becoming a number in the prison and taking us one step closer to twenty."

Once the guard had walked into the space in the middle of the barn, the crowd closed in, forming a tight circle around him and the two naked prisoners. Mistress returned to the top table.

"Three," the Queen called out and Flynn gulped. It suddenly felt much hotter in the barn.

"Two."

The prisoners looked at one another, the girl crying harder than ever.

"One."

The guard threw the chicken into the air and the crowd erupted into cheers.

Both Jason and his love ran around, hunched over as they tried to catch the fast bird. The crowd laughed at the absurdity of their nakedness, and when they crashed into one another—their heads connecting with a deep *tonk*—a deafening cheer damn near shook the walls of the place.

Because the guards and the Queen stood up to watch the prisoners, Flynn did the same. It wouldn't end well to openly challenge the woman on his left, so he played along. For now at least.

A few seconds later another loud roar crashed through the place. Flynn flinched from the volume of it while he watched Jason lift the chicken, his cock flapping around as he rose the dumb bird above his head.

"No," the girl said, her face buckling with her tears. "No, I can't go through the games. No, please."

A stony expression sat on the Queen's face as she stared at the girl. She spoke in a monotone. "Take her away."

If people made a noise around him at that moment, Flynn didn't notice. He could only hear the girl's screams as the guards dragged her out of there.

Chapter Fifty

They'd taken the girl from the barn, but Jason remained in the middle, the chicken still twisting and flapping against his tight grip.

Where Flynn would have expected a speech from the Queen, she said nothing. She didn't need to. It would seem Mistress knew her thoughts at that moment.

Mistress held her scimitar out in front of her as she moved back around the long table and walked down to Jason.

Sweat ran down Jason's pale face. He looked at Mistress and then her grinning weapon.

The community seemed to enjoy ceremony, certainly from what Flynn had seen so far. So it caught him completely off guard when Mistress grabbed Jason's manhood so hard he screamed, and cut it clean off with one swipe of her sword. No words, no preamble, just swift justice.

Jason yelled out, and what seemed like all the men in the room dragged a breath in through clenched teeth.

Mistress held the floppy appendage up at the Queen before she tossed it over her shoulder with a shrug and drove the tip of her blade through Jason's right eye.

It all happened so quickly Flynn's head spun.

Silence swept through the barn as Jason fell dead to the ground.

The Queen still said nothing, a slight grin on her otherwise stony face. She then turned to Flynn and patted his shoulder. "Why don't you go and get some rest, sweetheart?"

As he turned to leave the barn, the Queen added, "Jason was an energetic lad, you'll need to get your strength up if you're to match his stamina."

Chapter Fifty-One

The second Flynn woke up, he looked at his bedroom door. He somehow knew the Queen was watching him through the small round window, but it didn't stop him jumping from the shock of it.

A glazed look sat in the Queen's eyes. It sent a chill through him and he quickly covered himself with his duvet, despite the heat in the room.

Daylight shone in from outside. He'd either been asleep for a few hours, or he'd gone through an entire night. Because everything ached, he couldn't be sure either way.

The Queen stared in expectation at Flynn, who sat up in bed, reached down for his T-shirt, and pulled it on. The sting of his brand had already eased a little because of the cream she'd given him.

Taking his actions as an invitation, the Queen entered the room. Dressed in her usual tight-fitting black jeans and knee-high boots, she had her hair scraped back in an extreme ponytail. A cocked eyebrow and a half smile and she said, "Quite tired, then, I see? I'm not surprised, considering what you went through with the games. We've had plenty of times where no one's made it to the end because of how hard they are."

Although he looked at the Queen, Flynn thought about Rose. He quickly dropped his gaze to his lap so she didn't see the betrayal in his eyes. Especially since he'd seen what she'd done to Jason. "How long have I been asleep for?"

"Well, you left the barn yesterday lunchtime. I was going to wake you for dinner, but I thought better of it." A look down in the direction of his crotch and the slightest smile lifted one side of her mouth. "Better for you to get your strength up. You'll be needing it."

With an already dry mouth from sleeping in a hot room without a drink, Flynn fought the urge to gulp as he stared at her, his pulse speeding up. "So, uh, why have you woken me now?"

The Queen let the silence hang and stared straight at him. Lust glazed her stare and she looked to be considering what she'd do with him next. As if snapping out of it, she finally said, "We're going out."

Flynn relaxed a little, but tried to hide his relief. "Where are we going?"

"You'll see. As much as I don't want to say this, put some clothes on. I'll wait for you out in the hallway."

Chapter Fifty-Two

Fortunately they didn't expect Flynn to ride one of the horses. He'd never learned how. Instead, he sat on the back of the Queen's horse, yet again paying homage to her dominance over him.

About twenty horses in total, each one had two people on it. About thirty of them were the men under Mistress' command. The Queen had told him they were referred to as hunters. The other ten or so were the Queen's female guards. They rode the closest to them and all wore the same royal blue.

Several hours had passed since they'd left the royal complex. Flynn had grown beyond uncomfortable, the base of his back aching and his hips sore. Although it would ease some of his pain, he didn't want to wrap his arms around the Queen. He didn't need to be at any more of a submissive disadvantage with her—especially with the ravenous looks she gave him.

The Queen hadn't said anything to Flynn for the entire journey. Every time he'd thought about asking her where they were headed, she snapped at someone in the group for doing something wrong. It seemed wise to keep his mouth shut.

Besides, he hoped they were going to the town where they had Rose imprisoned, and any questioning would surely reek of his desire to save her. If he couldn't hide it from the Queen, then he shouldn't say it at all. A glance across at Mistress a few horses away and he saw the scimitar strapped to her hip. It had been cleaned of Jason's blood as if ready to remove another appendage.

And if they weren't heading to the town with Rose, he'd find out where they were going when they got there. Anything had to be better than her trying to fuck him. An attractive woman, but too old for him and far too domineering.

Just before the brow of the next hill, the Queen pulled her horse to a stop. She slipped to the ground and beckoned for Flynn to come down and join her.

Together they walked to the top of the hill and Flynn suddenly saw why. A decent-sized community stretched out in front of them. Smaller than both the royal complex and Home, it still looked to be the residence for about fifty people, maybe even a few more.

As far as fortification went, it had nothing on the royal complex or Home. A fence had been erected around it much like the ones used to contain livestock before everything went to hell. No more than a metre high, even a human would be able to hurdle it. The nomads tended to be bullies and would only pick battles they thought they could win. Flynn assumed this place had only managed to remain safe because of the number of people living there.

"So what are we doing here?" Flynn said as he watched some of the people in the community working the land.

"We're going to raid the place."

As much as he expected her to say that, Flynn's stomach still sank. The hunters around him drew their weapons. Some of them had longbows. Some had swords and axes for hand-to-hand combat. After he'd looked at them, he looked back at the Queen.

"We do well with our self-sufficient approach to things, but sometimes it's not enough. I have itches I need to scratch, and taking what I want, when I want, is one of those itches." She let the silence hang and stared at Flynn's crotch.

The Queen then stepped over the brow of the hill, revealing herself should anyone look her way. She beckoned Flynn forward with her. "Come on then, I need you with me."

Chapter Fifty-Three

The closer they got to the community, the more pathetic the fence around it looked. So low down, the long grass stood higher than it at most points. How the fuck had they lasted as long as they had without being raided? They'd been naive to think they could survive forever.

The grass dragged on Flynn's progress and the fresh smell of his surroundings wafted up at him. It offered a strange counterbalance to the rock in his stomach and the dread that seeped poison into his psyche.

"Let me put my arm around you," the Queen said to him.

As much as Flynn wanted to question it, he didn't.

The Queen feigned an injury and exaggerated a limp as she leaned into Flynn. They stumbled down the hill together, all the aches from his run through the games returning as he bore her weight.

Two flimsy corrugated tin gates stood at the front of the community. Like the fences next to them, they didn't look up to much and were only a few metres high.

Still about twenty metres from the place, a crack opened

between the two gates. A man and a woman stepped out. The man had a pitchfork, the woman a shovel.

"They look like fucking cavemen," the Queen muttered.

The two guards didn't speak. Instead, they stared at Flynn and the Queen and waited.

The Queen muttered beneath her breath to Flynn, her words sending ice through his veins. "We don't expect a body count from you today. Just watch and see how it's done."

As much as Flynn wanted to call out to the people in front of him, he didn't. A deep breath did little to settle the ever-tightening tension in him.

Maybe Flynn's fear of the Queen kept him quiet—after all, he'd seen her order multiple deaths. Maybe he wanted to make sure he got to Rose and rescued her; he owed her because of her sacrifice. Whatever the reason, he couldn't justify it. He knew what was about to happen and he wasn't about to do anything to stop it.

When the gap between them closed to no more than ten metres, the man stood straighter and pulled his shoulders back. "That's quite close enough," he said.

But the Queen pushed them forward several more steps as if trying to provoke him.

"I said that's quite close enough," the man repeated, his voice deepening as he brandished his pitchfork.

"I'm sorry," the Queen said. Flynn didn't recognise her weak and vulnerable voice. Meek like a nervous child, she continued, "I've injured my leg. We need somewhere to rest up for a day or two before we carry on."

The man shook his head. "We don't take people in. We

don't know who you are, and we have our families inside. We can't risk it."

A shake ran through Flynn and he did his best to control it.

"What about you, dear?" the Queen said to the woman. "This *man* makes all the decisions, does he?"

A slight flinch at her words, but the woman didn't bite. A tight jaw and she nodded. "It's like he said."

"Fair enough." The strength had already returned to the Queen's voice, even if she hadn't shown it with her body language yet. She then looked up at the sky and set a tongue-rolling battle cry free, the sharp call of it ringing out over the meadow surrounding the community.

In the time it took for the man and woman to look at one another, the twenty or so horses they'd brought with them galloped over the brow of the hill. Several arrows flew past Flynn and the Queen, so close Flynn felt the air shift next to his face. Every one embedded in the chests of the two guards.

It robbed the man and woman of their voices before they'd had a chance to use them. Both of them opened their mouths to release nothing but a gurgled sound.

The Queen let go of Flynn and straightened herself as the guards both fell over dead. A shake of her head as she stared down at them and laughed. "I suppose it wouldn't be any fun if they'd obliged us."

Chapter Fifty-Four

The second they stepped through the weak front gates, Flynn's eyes ran up the track leading away from him. The main thoroughfare, it had a couple of small buildings on either side of it near to them.

Farther away from them, Flynn saw a barn similar to that used by the Queen in the royal complex. As the main building in the place, they probably used it as a communal area too.

The people Flynn had seen working from the brow of the hill had vanished. Maybe they'd set up an ambush. Although, it seemed more than likely they were hiding. He looked at the barn again. They probably weren't hiding very well.

Crops grew on either side of the track between the two small huts and the barn. Other than that, Flynn couldn't see much else. Did they sleep in the barn too? Maybe the barn hid other structures behind it.

The Queen pointed at a flatbed trailer much like the ones they'd put spikes on for the games. At least three metres long, it looked to have been well maintained, the wooden wheels smooth and round, the flatbed repaired with different pieces of wood from where it had clearly broken over the years. "Grab that," she said to Flynn.

Almost every urge inside of Flynn screamed *no* at the woman. These people didn't deserve it. They seemed peaceful, like they just wanted to get on. Yet under her steely and psychotic glare, he did exactly as she ordered and walked over to the trailer, his shoulders slumped, his legs heavy.

When he brought the trailer back to the Queen—the squeaking of the wheels making the only sound as everyone watched him—she looked him up and down, lingering on his crotch. "Is there a problem?"

Jason's screams rang through Flynn's mind and he glanced over at Mistress' scimitar. He shook his head to look at the grinning weapon. "No, no problem at all."

"Right, follow me."

Mistress sat on the lead horse, her hunters and the Queen's royal blue guards behind her. They all waited for the Queen.

The Queen moved off and Flynn followed her, the wheels of the trailer squeaking again as he pulled it along with him. The entire party moved forwards at his pace, the horses stepping and then stopping, stepping and stopping.

The first two wooden huts looked like somewhere people would stay, but it seemed odd they were so far from the rest of the community. Unless they were guards' huts.

In response to several hand signals from the Queen, four of Mistress' hunters slipped from the back of their horses. The pillions on each horse, they left the riders behind as they moved forwards with their swords and bats at the ready.

The Queen directed two hunters to one hut and two to the other.

Flynn wanted no part of it. If he could have run, he would, but if he made a break for it, he probably wouldn't even make it to the gates before an arrow sank into his back. Besides, he couldn't outrun a horse even if he did get free.

Screams responded to the hunters entering the huts. Screams of what sounded like older larynxes—a younger, fitter person would have made more noise. It took until that moment for Flynn to notice the red crosses painted on the side of each hut. Clearly the community's hospital.

The hunters emerged seconds later. Two of them had a woman that looked to be in her eighties, and the other two, a man of a similar age. The couple looked tired and pale.

Maybe they were there before, but when Flynn looked up the track, he saw a gathering of people in the barn's doorway. They were crammed in the large space and all of them stared out.

A man with a beard and homemade sandals elbowed his way through the crowd to the front. "Please," he called out at the Queen. "*Please* let them be. They're both dying. We're keeping them in the hospital huts so we can give them palliative care. You can take our food, we can grow more, but please don't harm us."

The four hunters looked from the man to the Queen, who stared at the old people with a sneer on her face. The air wound so thick, Flynn damn near choked on it.

In a cold monotone, the Queen said, "Kill 'em."

Before the old people could scream, the hunters cut the sounds from their throats. One slice each and both fell at the same time, their weak frames making little noise as they folded to the ground, blood emptying from their deep wounds.

The community in the doorway cried and shouted. Chaos rushed out of the barn as everyone vocalised their grief at the same time.

When the bearded man stepped forward, everyone else quietened down. He threw his arms wide, his face red as he addressed the Queen. "What the fuck's wrong with you?"

Flynn looked at the Queen as she first glared at the man and then looked down at the dead bodies. "Right, you four." She pointed at the dismounted hunters as if the man from the community didn't exist. "I want you to follow behind and take everything that's useful. Flynn's going to pull the trailer while you load it up. And when you've been into each building, if you can find a torch, use it to burn them to the ground."

The hunters nodded and vanished into the hospital huts.

"Oi!" the man called again and stepped closer to the group. "I asked you a question, you crazy bitch."

Although Flynn looked at the Queen, he couldn't see any sign she'd even heard the man. Instead, she turned her back on him and spoke to the hunters and guards still on their horses. "The rest of you," she said, calmer than she'd ever sounded, "take 'em out."

The thunder of horse hoofs rattled past Flynn, trampling the dead people and sending an earthquake through the ground. The rush of their charge created a strong breeze in their wake.

Flynn watched the bearded man's anger turn to slack fear, his face falling south. A second later, one of the hunters on the back of the lead horse drove a hard blow with a baseball bat into the side of his head.

Chapter Fifty-Five

However long had passed, Flynn had lost track of time as everything turned into a blur. He walked back through the community, sweating and his muscles straining from dragging the now heavy trailer. He looked at the Queen. A sick pleasure lit her up.

The screams had died down as the people fell. The sound of the trailer's wheels creaked as Flynn tugged it. The air reeked of smoke and seared flesh. Much of the earth had turned damp with spilled blood.

"This is what we do," the Queen said as she looked at their stacked trailer. "Quite a good haul and a *wonderful* body count."

Not that Flynn had seen her kill anyone. He said nothing.

"Survival of the fittest," the Queen added, taking in the burning ruins around them.

Flynn had satisfied his curiosity as they delved deeper into the community. Many of the huts the community slept in were positioned behind the large barn, as he'd thought they might be. All of them were alight.

When they passed a dead child no older than five or six, a titter escaped the Queen. The boy's mouth hung wide open and his glassy eyes stared up at the sky. She clicked her fingers at a hunter and pointed at the boy. The hunter ran over, picked the boy up by his ankles, and launched him into a nearby fire.

A thick cloud of smoke wafted across Flynn and the Queen's path and he held his breath while it passed. The cloying cloud seemed to cling to him, sticking to his sweating skin like oil, wiping a stain of what he'd been a part of on him.

"We grow what we want, and we take what we want." The Queen spoke as if the lines had been rehearsed. As if she had no connection to them other than a rhetoric she hoped to believe if she repeated it enough times.

Flynn still didn't respond.

"You have to say something, Sixteen."

The mention of his number snapped tension through Flynn. She'd called him Flynn since he'd been in the community. She'd called him Flynn when she'd let him know she intended to fuck him. But maybe now, at the height of her bloodlust, she showed him what he was to her: a number that could be done away with at any moment.

"So," the Queen said, "are you in?"

A throat so dry he couldn't speak, Flynn nodded. What else could he do?

The Queen smiled, the same distant look in her psychotic gaze. "Good." Her tone dropped. "Next time you don't get to look away, okay?"

She'd seen him turn away. Flynn gulped the taste of smoke down and nodded.

"Now," the Queen said, "let's get this cart hooked up to one of the nags and head back to the royal complex. We'll be celebrating tonight."

Chapter Fifty-Six

Flynn rode pillion all the way back to the royal complex. Like on the way over, the Queen didn't speak much, which he felt more than happy to go along with. A darkness had taken her over when they were still in the sacked community. Everything that had come from her mouth since was brimming with the threat of violence.

The cart Flynn had pulled through the community had been tethered to the back of one of the horses. Its rider and passenger sat on the trailer and rocked with the rough ground as the cart rolled over it.

The wind raced across the open fields, kicking up the smell of horse sweat, human sweat, and blood. Maybe the blood had been ingrained into his psyche since the slaughter. He looked down at his shoes and the mud caking them. If he looked harder, he'd be bound to see the spilled essence of the villagers on them too.

When the huge wall of the royal complex came into view, Flynn released an involuntary gasp.

"Amazing, isn't it?" the Queen said. "I forgot you haven't returned here without a blindfold on."

It did look amazing. Something about seeing it revealed rather than riding away from it gave the complex its punch. The large tree-trunk fences, militant in their refusal to let anyone in who didn't belong. And the gates—not shitty corrugated tin like the community they'd left in flames, these gates only opened when the people of the royal complex intended them to.

Chapter Fifty-Seven

Well before they got to the gates, the sound of the large bolts cracked through the surrounding area and they were pulled open to allow the Queen and her party entry.

The huge hinges creaked and the people who'd remained behind formed two lines down either side of the path. They clapped and cheered as the Queen and her crew entered. Some played homemade drums and children danced. How many of them knew the sacrifices that had been made to bring the stack of food back to them?

Even Flynn—who was no more than the Queen's intended plaything—got a rousing welcome for his return.

To look at the people joyous in their celebrations made Flynn's head spin. How had the Queen become their ruler? Although, like with Brian, Sharon, and Dan, she offered them stability. Sell people the illusion of security and they'd hand over their freedom.

Once the hunters and their horses had entered the royal complex and come to a halt, Flynn slipped from the back of the Queen's horse and held his hand out to help her down.

Although she didn't seem like someone to take help, she took it nonetheless, slid from her horse, and continued to hold his hand. She kept a firm grip. A grip that told him who called the shots.

Today would drag on, the celebrations no doubt lasting for hours. Maybe it would be the best day to get the fuck away from the bunch of lunatics. Sure, Rose still sat trapped in a dungeon, but what chance did he have of rescuing her anyway? He had no idea where they kept her and the Queen probably wouldn't reveal it to him any time soon.

Flynn leaned close enough to the Queen so only she would hear. He whispered in her ear, "I need to go back to my room."

The Queen spun on him, her face locked in a scowl.

"I need to clean up," he said. "Dragging that cart took its toll on me, so I want to go and bathe. I'd like to be clean for you later."

The Queen's demeanour changed, her back straightening as she smiled slightly. "Well, when you put it like that … We'll eat in about half an hour. Is that enough time for you?"

"Plenty." Flynn lifted her hand and kissed the back of it. "I'll rush."

And with that he spun on his heel and headed back to his room. Rose had no hope, so he had to get out of there while he still had a chance.

Chapter Fifty-Eight

Flynn entered his room, pushed the door firmly closed behind him, and walked straight to the window. It let light in but didn't look like it had been cleaned in years. Dirt tinted the glass, dulling his view of the outside world.

Before now it had been no more than a source of light. A cursory glance at the view when he'd first walked into the room and Flynn saw nothing to get excited about. Because of that he hadn't looked out of it much. Besides, whenever he'd been in his room, he'd either been washing or sleeping; there hadn't been much time for anything else.

Now Flynn had a reason to look out of the window. He'd seen the overgrown courtyard the first time he'd looked, but now he gave it more of his attention. Several rooms overlooked the ugly space. How many of the other residents had taken the time to look at it?

Paving slabs were arranged with gravel patches in between like a chessboard. The patches looked like they could have been flowerbeds if someone had been bothered to give the space that love and care. Grass grew up through the gaps.

An old metal box at least two metres high stood along one side of the small courtyard. Flynn had seen similar things in similar buildings. Vicky had told him they had been used for power or air-conditioning or communications.

Old, ugly, and obsolete, the tall metal structure would be the perfect step up onto the hospital's roof. If Flynn got up there unnoticed, he could reach the royal complex's wall and get the fuck away. Thirty minutes would give him enough time to be gone for good. No way would they catch him after that.

When Flynn thought about Rose, the guilt inside him grew claws. But realistically, what could he do for her now? She probably wouldn't even make it from the dungeon. And from the way the Queen behaved with her erratic bipolar mood swings, he probably wouldn't be alive by the time she got out anyway.

Flynn pressed against the window. It didn't budge. When he looked down, he saw two small holes where a handle had once been bolted to it. They'd made sure he couldn't get out. "Fuck."

Adrenaline sent Flynn's heart rate off the charts as he paced his room. The tick of seconds slipped away from him. He had this chance, he had to make the most of it, and he had to make it work. If he tried to escape and failed … The memory of Jason's scream rang through his mind. He had to make it work.

He'd wrap something around his hand, smash the window as quietly as he could, and then get out of there. If he moved quickly, it would work. He'd make it work.

They'd left a towel for him when he first came into the community. It currently hung over the chair near his bath. Flynn picked it up, and just before he could wrap it around his fist, a heavy knock clattered on his door.

The bang of it sent Flynn's pulse racing and he spun around to see the Queen's face peering in through the round window. The smile felt almost painful, but he forced it anyway. "Hi. Come in."

She snapped the handle of his door down hard, like she wanted to break it clean off, like her sexual frustration drove her every action. She stormed into the room. For a moment she stared at him and the towel in his hand. "Don't you need to get wet before you use a towel?"

"I was just moving it so I could run a bath. Is everything okay?"

"I need to take you out again."

"Already?"

"Something urgent's come up."

"So urgent that I can't wash first?"

The now familiar cock of an eyebrow and she stared at him. The veiled threat dared him to push it.

"Okay," Flynn said with a sigh. "I can wash later."

The Queen didn't respond. Instead, she stormed from the room and Flynn followed her out.

Chapter Fifty-Nine

Flynn rode pillion again. Of course he did. Like before, no one spoke as they made their way across the grassy fields. The place would have looked so different twenty years ago. The frail corpses of buildings stood on the skyline, painting a picture of what used to be. Cars would have driven down the broken and grassy road they currently travelled along.

When they left the royal complex, the sky had been clear. Now clouds covered the vast blue expanse. The humidity had turned up several notches and Flynn sweated where he sat. His T-shirt clung to his back and the brand above his right kidney, although sore, felt much better for the cream he'd put on it. Half a tube down, hopefully they'd give him more when he ran out. If he hadn't gotten away by then.

The sway of the horse forced Flynn to constantly move so he didn't fall off. It sweated almost as much as he did and his trousers had turned damp with it. It would have been much easier to hold onto the Queen for stability, but he wouldn't do that. No way.

The Queen's guards had come out with them. Four horses

on either side of them, each had two guards on. Eight royal blue women.

Mistress and several of her hunters had joined them too. It all amounted to Flynn giving up on the idea of escape for the time being.

Were it just him and the Queen, he would have killed the bitch and been long gone. Too much longer around these lunatics and he'd go nuts. Especially with what she had planned for him.

"So where did you say we're going?" Flynn finally asked, breaking the muted atmosphere and pulling the attention of everyone onto him.

"I didn't," the Queen replied as she continued to stare straight ahead. "You need to be more patient. I hope you're not as eager in other departments." She reached back and clamped a strong hand on his thigh, her fingers stinging as they dug in. "Maybe I'll find out. Maybe not. Jason was *very* eager, you know."

A look at the others and Flynn met their dead stares. They knew where they were going. They knew what would happen to him.

The Queen spoke again. "I want to show you something."

Several of the hunters flashed predatory grins at Flynn, but he didn't ask any more questions.

A cool breeze ran over the fields, bending the long grass and cooling Flynn's sweating skin. It brought a fresh smell with it, clearing the stink of horse momentarily.

Movement from Mistress' hunters and Flynn saw several of them draw their weapons. They pulled their horses to a stop, as did the others.

"Get off," the Queen said.

A look from the Queen to Mistress' hunters and back to the Queen, and Flynn said, "Why?"

"What's with the questions?"

Despite the cooler breeze, a hot wave of nausea rose up in Flynn. When he saw Mistress' hunters slip from their steeds, he did the same.

The Queen remained on her horse, the wind flicking her long black hair. She stared down at Flynn, zero emotion in her cold expression. "We have something for you."

Six of Mistress' hunters had dismounted and all of them brandished their weapons as they formed a tight circle around Flynn. At first, he spun and looked at the one closest to him, then the one next to him, then ... Once he'd turned several complete circles, each hunter levelling a steely glare at him, he looked up at the Queen. She watched on with her usual detachment. "What have I done wrong?"

The hunters closed in another few inches.

At that moment, the clouds above split and the first drops of rain hit Flynn's bare arms. He looked up at the ominous sky, gunmetal grey stretching out above them. It took all he had not to piss himself where he stood.

"Wait," the Queen said to the hunters and she slid from her horse. The men parted for her as she walked over to Flynn, her dark stared fixed on him. "Let *me* do this."

Chapter Sixty

A small bag hung from the Queen's belt. Flynn hadn't noticed it until now. More a pouch than a bag, it lifted away from her hip as she walked and patted against it again. She slipped her hand into it as she stepped into the ring of hunters and drew out a pair of binoculars.

Flynn stared down at them. "Huh?"

"Expecting something more deadly?"

He didn't respond.

"Come with me," the Queen said.

The ring of hunters parted to let them out. They closed in tighter as Flynn followed after the Queen, just to make it more uncomfortable for him. Despite the rain now falling, the men still smelled of sweat—horses' and their own.

They'd stopped just before the brow of a nearby hill, much like they'd done when they came to the community they'd raided earlier that day. Maybe she didn't plan on killing him. Whatever she planned on doing, she had control. So many guards and hunters around them, Flynn couldn't sneeze without feeling cold steel between his shoulder blades.

The Queen handed Flynn her binoculars and said, "This is what we've come here for." She led him forward.

The air left Flynn's lungs even before he saw it. They'd approached it from an angle he hadn't approached it from before; otherwise he might have twigged sooner.

"Beautiful, ain't it?"

What could he say? "Um, yeah. What is this place?"

The Queen moved so close to him they were touching shoulders, and the rain fell harder than ever. "I dunno," she said. "We didn't know about it until just recently. One of my hunters found it. But it looks like it has something worth taking, right?"

Maybe she knew. "Yeah," Flynn said, "it certainly looks that way."

"I need your help sussing the place out. We need to work out the best way to attack them."

Flynn nodded, his throat dry.

"And maybe we'll come back in a few days with a decent-sized army and roll right over them. They look like they might be harder to take down than the last place."

She must have known. It all had to be a part of her twisted game. But Flynn had to play along. "I think we need to get closer so we can see the place better," he said and stepped down the hill, keeping low so the grass hid him.

Mistress followed behind.

"What are those things there?" Flynn said, pointing down to the new community and handing the Queen her binoculars back.

After she'd looked through them, she pulled them away and said, "They look like tubes and pipes of some sort. Maybe some way to catch water."

"I reckon we should make a hole in their fence and attack them by coming through that way."

The Queen patted Flynn on the back, the slap of her hand stinging against his wet T-shirt. "That sounds like a good plan."

Together they turned their backs on Home and returned to the others.

"We're going to come back in a few days," the Queen said, "and take everything they have from them."

Watched by the guards and hunters, Flynn kept his mouth shut.

Chapter Sixty-One

The rain had fallen hard on their ride back to the royal complex. It left Flynn unable to justify having a bath. The bathwater was no cleaner than rainwater.

Even now, sat in the barn with the rest of the community, Flynn's bare arms stung from the lashing the rain had given him on their ride. It still fell hard, pelting the roof while the community ate in the sweaty space.

While chewing her food, the Queen leaned close to Flynn, breathing the stench of her meal on him. "I reckon we should check out that community a few more times before we raid them. What do you think?"

Flynn's mouthful caught in his throat and he gulped several times to pull it down before he nodded. Heat flushed his cheeks and the humidity in the hot barn made him sweat.

The Queen stared at Flynn, her eyes boring into the side of his face. "What did you say the place was called?"

The word *Home* rushed to the edge of Flynn's tongue, but he caught it before it slipped free. He hadn't said its name to her. "Huh?" he said because he had nothing else.

Fire burned through Flynn's face to feel the Queen stare at him, but she didn't reply.

Whatever happened between now and when they went to raid Home, Flynn needed to get the fuck away. Just because he hated a few people at Home, he couldn't make the entire community suffer. Maybe he couldn't stop the Queen and her band of murderous arseholes, but he didn't have to play any part in it.

When the Queen clapped her hands next to Flynn, he jumped as the sharp crack of it silenced the place. She got to her feet and said, "Time for some more entertainment."

A rock sank through Flynn's stomach. He gripped his knife. If he had to, he'd take her down before they could do anything to him. Better to attack one of them than none.

But he wasn't the entertainment today. Instead, the doors opened and in walked a topless girl. She had a hood over her head and wore a grass skirt. A hunter walked in behind her with a drum.

The people in the barn cleared a space in the middle like they had before. The hunter led the girl into it. She had a collar around her neck. A chain ran from it to the hunter's belt.

In the centre of the room, the hunter whipped the girl's hood away and Flynn instantly lost his appetite. As before, he felt the Queen's glare burning into him and he tried his hardest to suppress his reaction. As before, his face burned like it had been set fire to.

"Well?" the Queen said.

There seemed little point in hiding it. "I was sure I wouldn't see her again," Flynn replied as he stared at Rose. "I didn't think the dumb bitch would make a third run through the games."

Calling Rose a dumb bitch seemed to tickle the Queen. She threw her head back and laughed at the wooden ceiling. Then, as quickly as her laughter had exploded from her, it fell and she clicked her fingers at the drummer. "Play."

Not much of a musician, the drummer played a steady beat.

The Queen turned her attention on Rose. "Dance."

As tempting as it was to look at her, Flynn ignored Rose and focused on his meal. Every gulp went down like jagged rocks, but he pushed through it, flinching every time the Queen laughed next to him. He couldn't be a part of Rose's humiliation, but he couldn't do much to help her either. The sooner this evening ended, the better.

Chapter Sixty-Two

Flynn peered out through his bedroom window into the darkness of the hospital's corridor. It had to be late enough. The only light came from the moon. Everyone had to be sleeping by now. It had to be late enough.

The Queen hadn't called Flynn to her room that night, but she would one of these evenings soon. And she could still beckon him now. The crazy bitch got drunk on her power, so it wouldn't surprise him if she saw fit to call on him in the middle of the night. Wake him up just so he could fuck her.

Flynn needed to find Rose. He owed her. When she'd been hidden in a secret location miles from where he stayed, he could pretend nothing could be done. But now, with her in the same community as him, he had to find her and he had to help her. When he did, they could both get out of there.

In the still of night, even the creak of Flynn's door handle went off like cannon fire. Would the Queen have someone watching him? Were they waiting for him to go to Rose so she could cut his cock off in front of everyone? He couldn't second-guess anyone or anything. Rose needed his help and they both needed to get the fuck away from the twisted community.

Up until that point, Flynn had turned right when leaving his room. Right led out of the hospital. This time he turned left. There had to be more rooms to the left.

Fortunately, the moon shone through the dark corridor's skylights. Bright enough to make shadows of obstacles, Flynn managed to avoid the things in his path with relative ease.

A glance through each round window as he passed them. Flynn found most of the rooms to be empty. Maybe he'd see the Queen in one of them.

The next door benefitted from being directly beneath a skylight in the corridor. It lit it up enough to show him the difference between this room and all of the others he'd seen. This one had a lock on the outside. A cell rather than a bedroom.

Flynn's heart pounded as he looked both up and down the corridor. If he returned to his room now, no one would be any the wiser. But he'd have to remain in the royal complex. He'd have to turn his back on Rose after she'd saved his life. He couldn't do that. Now he'd left his room, he couldn't ever return.

When Flynn got closer to the door, he peered inside. Unlike his room, this room had mattresses spread over the floor. Each mattress had a sleeping form on it. They looked like women, but he couldn't be sure. It could have been small men. Or children. He hadn't seen any children in the royal complex. He'd have to go in to find out.

While holding his breath, Flynn pinched the cold bolt securing the door, his hand shaking. He bit down on his bottom lip as he wiggled it up and down, easing the stiff lock gently free.

Every few seconds, he looked both ways along the corridor. From what he saw, it remained clear of people. Yet the skin on the back of his neck crawled as imagined eyes burned into him. A spectator in the dark waiting for the right moment to reveal themselves.

The lock let out a light click as it came free and Flynn released his breath. One last look up and down the corridor and he slipped into the room.

Chapter Sixty-Three

The rain had stopped a few hours previously, so the only noise Flynn heard in the dark room came from the rhythmic breathing as the women slept. At least, he assumed all of them were women. It felt like a room full of women.

Still too dark to tell if Rose lay amongst them, Flynn had to check one woman at a time. It made sense to start with the closest to the door.

Flynn's body still ached from the exertion of the past few days, so when he hunched down next to the first sleeping woman, pain groaned through him.

She slept with her back to Flynn. Her shirt rose up a little, revealing her brand. Over her left kidney, Flynn saw the number one. First time! He'd found her on the first time of trying.

Flynn gripped Rose's shoulder and gave it a gentle shake. "Rose," he whispered, "it's me, Flynn."

Despite there being very little light in the room, Rose squinted as if blinded by a glare. The confusion of sleep quickly left her when she looked at Flynn and her face fell. She shook her head and sighed. "Oh, Flynn, I wish you hadn't come."

Because he'd been so focused on Rose, Flynn hadn't seen the movement around him. When he looked up, he saw every other woman in the room had risen to their feet. Each one of them brandished a sword.

The slow sound of clapping came down the corridor towards the room and Flynn shook to hear it. It cracked in time with her heavy-booted steps.

What seemed like an age passed and the repeated clap chipped away at Flynn's resolve. Each sharp snap wound the muscles in his back a little bit tighter.

Then the Queen appeared in the doorway. Her head cocked to one side, she sighed as she said, "What a shame. I was kind of hoping you'd be different. All I want is someone to adore me, Flynn."

"Why the fuck would I adore a murderous maniac like you? You're fucking mental."

Silence seemed to sweep through the entire building as if the old hospital itself had drawn a breath. The Queen let it hang before she looked at her guards. "You know what to do."

The women closed in around Flynn and Rose.

Chapter Sixty-Four

Flynn spent the entire night rubbing his wrists together. The rope had been tied so tightly he didn't get any movement from them at first, and his hands throbbed from the circulation having been cut off. But the more he moved them, the more his bonds loosened.

The process had rubbed the skin off his wrists and they stung with an aggressive buzz, but he had to keep going. He'd already been through plenty of pain, a little more wouldn't stop him now.

Neither Flynn nor Rose spoke to one another. They seemed to share a fear that someone would be listening. At least that was what Flynn assumed to be Rose's reason for remaining quiet. He could only guess at what went through her mind at that moment.

At least they'd been trapped in the summer. Had they been left in what equated to a human birdcage in the winter, they would have probably gotten hypothermia from the first night.

Although summer brought its own challenges. Every time Flynn swallowed, his dry and swollen tongue damn near choked him. The rain had stopped quite a few hours ago, and he hoped it would start up again soon; both his wrists and his throat could do with the wet relief.

The cage hung from the branch of the only large tree in the royal complex. It stood close to the barn, and when the people of the community woke up, Flynn and Rose would be in plain sight.

The silence chipped away at Flynn, so he finally said, "I'm worried they're going to cut my dick off."

Rose frowned at him.

"She did that, you know. She had me lined up to be her fuck toy. The last guy who didn't make the grade had his penis cut off in front of everyone in the barn. The spectators loved it. They're fucking savages in this place."

"Fuck," Rose said as she looked at the large wooden structure close by. What else could she say? No doubt her mind spun like Flynn's. If the Queen would cut his dick off, what would she do to Rose?

Not only had Flynn's and Rose's wrists been bound, but they'd been anchored to a large metal ring in the middle of the birdcage. The angle Flynn had to sit at—hunched over and leaning forwards—set his shoulders on fire with a deep ache. Although he rolled them to try to ease his pain, it had little effect other than sending the birdcage swinging.

Some of the royal complex's early risers woke with the sun. Some completely ignored Flynn and Rose, while others stopped beneath the cage and stared up at them. No one spoke to them. And why would they? The wrong question at the wrong time in this place and the consequences were severe.

The first hunter Flynn saw came over to the cage and stood beneath it. It seemed to make the other people braver, many of them joining him in looking up at the pair.

About fifteen people had gathered by the time the hunter did something. After looking on the ground, he bent down and picked up an object. So tired from his sleepless night, Flynn didn't react as he watched the hunter's rock spin through the air at him. It cracked him straight on the forehead, sending a flash of white light through his vision. A hot line of blood ran into Flynn's right eye from the wound and he rubbed his head on his shoulder to try to stem the flow.

"You horrible fucker," the hunter called up at Flynn.

The hunter's actions gave the others permission, and in a few short seconds, the people below all launched rocks at the pair.

Flynn lowered his head as pain dashed his body. Each time a rock hit, the sharp sting of it felt all the worse for the surprise of where it crashed into him. His shoulder blades, his spine, the back of his head … Insults flew up at the pair with the rocks.

"Cunt," "Faggot," "Traitors," "Arseholes …"

Chapter Sixty-Five

The stoning lasted for about five minutes before the hunter called out, "Enough!"

The people stopped and Flynn opened one eye to look down to be sure they weren't tricking him. When he looked at Rose, he saw cuts and marks on her head and face. He balled his fists, clenched his jaw, and continued to rub his wrists together. They'd fucking pay. The lot of them would pay.

The hunter pointed up at the pair and said, "The Queen has plans for these lovebirds, so we can't be too harsh." The crowd around him were animated with their excitement. Their eyes as wide as their grins, they stared bloodlust up at Flynn and Rose.

"I can see you want to kill these two," the hunter said. "Believe me, they deserve it, but we need to wait. Whatever we can think to do to them, I'm sure the Queen has something *much* worse planned."

Of course the Queen had plans for them, but to hear it said out loud sent a nauseating flip through Flynn's guts. He rubbed his wrists together quicker than before.

When the hunter and the people had walked away, Flynn

looked at Rose. The same beauty he'd seen in her clean skin, her long blonde hair, and her brown eyes remained. Despite the welts and lumps from the stoning, her spirit shone through as bright as ever. She didn't look anywhere near as scared as he felt. "Why did you save me at the end of the games?"

Rose dropped her attention to the ring they were both bound to, her face flushing red. "You seemed like a good person. You seemed worth saving."

"But you could have saved yourself."

"I know. And maybe I would if we were to do it all again. I suppose at the time, I couldn't willingly sell you out. I couldn't be that ruthless."

Would Flynn have been that ruthless?

"But it's paid off, hasn't it?" Rose said.

Flynn looked down at the rope around his wrists, the sandy-coloured cord stained red with his blood. He blinked against the sweat and blood running into his eyes before he looked back up at Rose. "Um, no. I don't think it has paid off."

"You came to rescue me. We're in this together now. We'll work something out."

She'd been kind enough to save him, so Flynn didn't say anything, but they were fucked. No matter which way he looked at it, they were well and truly fucked. And the look in Rose's eyes told him she believed that too, even if she couldn't voice it.

Flynn's entire body buzzed like an open wound, although no part of it hurt more than his wrists. Even still, he continued to rub them together, each movement ever so slightly loosening the rope's tension.

Chapter Sixty-Six

Flynn now wore gloves of blood. They glistened in the sun, slick and red. Yet he continued to twist and turn them, gaining a little more slack out of the ropes with each passing hour. If it came to it, he'd rather lose a hand escaping than have that cunt Mistress cut his cock off.

The pain from the stoning still throbbed through Flynn, and as the day heated up, sweat turned his entire form damp. The saline trickle found every open wound on his body, lighting him up with an electric buzz.

Fuck knew how long had passed since they were stoned. The sun had risen higher in the sky. A lot more people had woken up, walked past the cage, and stared up at them. No one had spoken to them. No doubt they'd decide to stone them again at some point.

A clenched jaw against his pain and Flynn continued to work his wrists. The movement of his hands continued to send the cage swinging. So when he saw the Queen approach, he stopped still.

"Well, well, well," the Queen said, three royal blue guards

on either side of her. "Two little lovebirds. Caged, as lovebirds should be. You know, apparently lovebirds fall in love for life. If they're separated, it breaks the other one's heart."

Neither Flynn nor Rose responded as the Queen evaluated them with her cold glare. "I have plans for the both of you. I expect one of you will end up heartbroken." She smiled. "But we have a little time yet, so don't worry."

Flynn did his best to keep his eyes from his burning wrists. Because the bottom of the cage was made from solid wood, they'd have to lower it to see what he'd been trying to do.

"But before anything else happens," the Queen said, "we have a community to raid. Isn't that right, Flynn?"

Still silent, Flynn looked down at the Queen and the ravenous faces of her guards. Hungry for his utter destruction, they looked ready to pounce.

"*Home*, is that what it's called?"

The word sent a chill through Flynn. Sure, he'd walked away from the place, washed his hands of it even, but only because of a select few people. Many of Home's residents hadn't done anything to him. He'd devoted over a decade of his life to ensuring the well-being of the place; he'd like it to continue to thrive.

And how did she know about Home? He'd told her he came from Biggin Hill, from the shipping containers. Flynn searched the crowd of spectators below, which had doubled since the Queen arrived. A sharp sting sat in his eyes from the sweat and blood that had trickled into them over the past few hours. Maybe someone from Home now lived in the royal complex. How else would she know?

"I won't keep you any longer," the Queen said, "but I promise you, even from here, you'll be able to watch your old community burn. If you survive that long without food and water, that is. I still haven't decided on exactly when we'll take the place down."

Such a dry mouth it felt like his throat would crack, Flynn watched the Queen saunter off as she said, "Ta-ta."

Chapter Sixty-Seven

It must have been lunchtime, because as soon as the Queen left Flynn and Rose, she headed for the barn.

Over the course of the next five minutes or so, Flynn watched all the people from the community file into the large building. All the while, he twisted his wrists, rested a little to let the pain ease, and twisted again. A pool of blood had formed on the base of the cage from where it dripped off his fingers like melting wax.

"I'm worried about you," Rose said.

Flynn looked at her to see she had her attention on his wrists. A shrug of his shoulders and he continued to twist his hands. "Anything's got to be better than waiting up here for that bitch to decide when she's going to start toying with us."

The bright glare bounced off Rose's sweating face. Hotter than it had been in weeks, Flynn almost heard the sizzle of her skin from the sun's burn.

"So you come from the next community she wants to take down?"

"I did."

"Why did you leave?"

Flynn wanted to yell out at the pain in his wrists as he twisted them again, but he clenched his jaw, drew heavy breaths, and said, "They were cunts."

When Rose didn't reply, Flynn looked up at her. "I'm sorry," he said. "They *were* arseholes though."

Rose shrugged; this world had clearly shown her much worse than the word *cunt*. "What did they do?"

"I arrived there about a decade ago with a woman who raised me. She was like a mother to me. I was only six when my parents died. Were it not for her, I'd be dead too, a million times over."

"What happened to her?"

"She was murdered. By the people of Home."

Near silence hung between them, the creaking of the tree's branch the only sound as they rocked in the wind.

"I'm sorry to hear that," Rose finally said as she reached out two of her fingers on her right hand and stroked Flynn's. If their bonds would have allowed more contact, Flynn felt sure she would have given it to him at that moment; and he would have welcomed it.

As he looked down at her affection, some of Flynn's rage left him and a lump rose in his throat. "She was the one who helped set the disease loose on the world."

"*What?*"

"Someone used her because she had access to the tower where they were making the disease. She compromised the security of the place so they could get in. They convinced her they would put a stop to the experiments. She thought she was helping. But the people of Home didn't want to hear that. They only cared that she'd helped set the plague loose." As much as Flynn wanted to tell Rose he'd been the one who had spoken out about Vicky setting the virus loose, he didn't. That confession would go to the grave with him.

A kindness Flynn hadn't seen since Serj died stared at him from Rose's soft face. "I only found out a week or two back about them killing her, even though they did it ten years ago. She managed to persuade them to let her write me a letter to say she'd left. I was sixteen at the time and she knew if I found out about her being killed, I'd go off on my own. I wouldn't have lasted two minutes."

"So she'd rather you thought she left you than know the truth?"

"So I'd stay, yeah."

"Wow. It sounds like she saved your life, even if she couldn't save her own."

For the next few seconds, Flynn worked the bonds harder than before, rubbing and rubbing and rubbing, grinding his jaw against the pain of it. "A man named Serj looked after me once Vicky had gone. He knew the truth of it all, but he didn't tell me until just recently. He promised her he wouldn't."

"What made him break his promise?"

"He died."

"*Fuck!*"

"He wanted me to know Vicky didn't abandon me. A decade on and I was still so angry with her. I think he wanted to help me get over it. The thing is the people who killed her run Home. I couldn't stay there. Especially as I'd just split up with my girlfriend."

"Fucking hell," Rose said. "That's rough."

Flynn nodded. "Yeah, but everyone's had it hard, haven't they? That's what life is now."

"I suppose."

"And what about you? I'll be honest, you sounded fucking mental when you said everything's worked out because we're together." A shock of pain ran up both of Flynn's wrists when he twisted them again and he pulled a breath in through his clenched teeth.

"I was born to a heroin-addicted mother and came out of the womb with a habit," Rose said. "I was just two when the disease broke out. My mum hadn't gotten clean yet. Within five minutes of the disease spreading, my dad had turned into one of those *things*. He left a junkie and her kid all alone, not that he would have been any help anyway. He was better to us as a creature. At least it gave us the impetus to leave him."

Flynn let her continue.

"We lived in a basement for about six years. The only daylight I saw came through the crack in a wooden door. I would press my face against it for hours on end just so I could imagine what it would be like to live outside. We started with twelve of us down there. By the time we left, just Mum and I remained."

A cheer came from the dining hall and Flynn flinched, spinning around to look over at the barn. No one came out. He continued to wring his wrists. They had to get out of there before the Queen decided they were done.

"There were still diseased about, as you know," Rose said. "But far fewer than before. The communities that remained knew how to survive. A community took us in. And things were great for the longest time. But my community—as good as they were at being self-sufficient—weren't fighters. When there were no more diseased to fight, people started hunting people. About a year ago, our community was overrun. They killed all the men in the place and ate them"—Rose looked at the ground and spoke in a quieter voice—"in front of us. They took the women away with them."

Several deep breaths and Rose looked out over the royal complex. Her deep brown eyes glazed as she stared over the farmland and the high fence. "Before they could do anything to me or Mum, Mum attacked them and told me to run. I did. I ran and I didn't look back."

"So why are you still so hopeful we'll be okay? Especially with all the fucked-up shit you've witnessed."

"Because I'm still alive. *We're* still alive. In spite of everything, we're still here. I miss my mum every single day, but I'm not dead yet. I've had impossible situations and walked away from them, so why can't we do it again?"

Maybe she had a point. Another cheer came from the barn and Flynn doubled his efforts, grimacing through the pain in his wrists as he continued to twist and turn them. Maybe she had a point.

Chapter Sixty-Eight

Flynn did his best to hide away from the next stoning. He pulled his shoulders up and arched his back towards the people below. But the rocks came at him from every direction, and with his hands tied to the floor of the cage, he could only do so much to protect himself.

Although a lot of the projectiles hit him, many more didn't. They clattered into the bars of the cage and the base of it. The insults came as freely as the missiles.

"Scumbags."

"Fuckers."

"Traitors."

"Rats."

Every ten seconds or so, one of the rocks crashed into Flynn's head. It spun his entire world and it felt like the next one would knock him out.

Impossible for Flynn to tell because of his restricted movement, but it felt like cuts had opened up all over his body.

"Okay!" the Queen called and the stoning stopped. "It's dinnertime; let's leave them for a while."

Although Flynn listened to her cruel voice, he didn't look down at her. No way would he give the bitch the satisfaction of seeing him in pain. No fucking way.

"We'll come back tomorrow," the Queen said. "We need to be careful we don't kill them. We don't want to give them that relief too early." The people around the Queen laughed.

Flynn remained hunched over and listened to everyone walk away. When he sensed that most, if not all, of the people had entered the barn, he looked up at Rose. "Are you okay?"

Blood ran down her face from a deep gash on her forehead. She winced and nodded. "Yeah, I think so. A bit sore, but I don't think anything's broken."

"This can't go on," Flynn said. "We won't last many more stonings." He looked over at the barn. The doors were closed, but Mistress stood on the outside. It looked like everyone else had gone in. "I wonder what she's doing?" he said.

Rose looked over too but didn't respond.

The ropes around Flynn's wrists had more give now than ever, his hands slick with blood and sweat. The deep cuts he'd burned into them were on fire like red ants crawled beneath his skin. A look at Rose and he said, "I think this will be our best opportunity."

Flynn clenched his jaw and pulled against his bonds. Damn near blinding pain sent bright flashes through his vision. It felt like shaving the skin from his hands as he tugged again, harder than before. But he had to be brave. They had to get out of there.

Sweat ran into Flynn's sore eyes, but he continued to pull and pull against his bonds. He shook as he held onto his need to cry out and his hands slipped up a little way, then a little way more, then … Suddenly he pulled himself free.

Flynn lifted his hands and looked at the cuts to his skin. Blood ran down his forearms and two bangle-like flaps had lifted away around his wrists. They ran so deep he'd probably see the bone if he tried. He didn't want to try.

What little feeling Flynn had left in his hands enabled him to pull on Rose's ropes, clumsy as he shook and bled over them.

After a minute or two, he'd worked the rope free.

Rose pulled her hands out, wrapped Flynn in a tight hug, kissed him on the cheek, and quickly put her hands back to the base of the cage. They couldn't risk Mistress seeing them.

Chapter Sixty-Nine

Much more subtle in her movements the second time, Rose lifted both of Flynn's hands. His heart rate sped, and he did his best to hold onto his quickened breaths.

Gently, as if lifting an injured butterfly, she frowned like his wounds were her own. "I'm so sorry you've had to do this to yourself."

Rose then lifted the bottom of her shirt up to her mouth. Not the first time Flynn had seen her pert breasts, and maybe he shouldn't have looked. For the briefest moment he forgot his pain.

Her actions suddenly became clear when Rose bit a tear into the fabric at the bottom of her shirt and tore a strip free. The sound made both of them look over at Mistress, who seemed oblivious to what they were doing.

Rose clamped her top teeth on her bottom lip, all of her focus seemingly on Flynn's hands as she wrapped his right wrist in her makeshift bandage.

Although she pulled it tight and the pain sent Flynn slightly woozy, he let her continue. It felt like the correct thing to do.

Once Rose had finished with his right wrist, she did the same with his left.

Flynn glanced back at Mistress again. They were far enough away to be invisible to her. As long as they didn't make any sudden movements to attract her attention, they'd be fine.

"This'll help keep them free from infection," Rose said as she held onto his two bound wrists. They were wrapped from his forearm to his palm.

Rose lowered his hands and Flynn reciprocated in the only way he could think of. He reached up and wiped the blood away from the wound on her head.

The pair stared at one another as Flynn tucked her long blonde hair behind her ear.

It took for the hinges creaking on the barn door to break them out of it. They both turned to watch Mistress vanish inside.

"Right," Flynn said. "This is our chance."

Chapter Seventy

The cage hadn't seemed very sturdy at any point. More a prison because their hands were tied to the floor than because of its strong design. One of the wooden bars behind Flynn had several deep chips gouged into it from the stones that had been launched at them. He spun around so he had his back to Rose, lifted his right foot, and kicked out.

Two bars flew away from Flynn's very first kick, the wood falling to the ground with a clatter. Fuck knew if anyone heard it or not, but they couldn't worry about that now. They had to get out of there.

Despite the pain in his wrists, Flynn lay on his front, dropped his legs through the gap he'd just made, and eased himself out until he hung down from the cage. It left him just a couple of metres to fall.

The second Flynn hit the ground, he crumpled into a heap. His right foot turned beneath him from where he landed on a small rock.

Although Flynn's ankle hurt, he hadn't broken anything. He stood up and watched Rose hang down like he had and used his feet to sweep her landing area clear of the large stones.

Rose landed with the grace of a cat.

After he'd checked she was okay, Flynn turned and headed for the barn.

"What are you doing?" Rose said.

"I can't let them attack Home. Especially since I've seen what they do to the communities they raid. That can't happen." He didn't look around to see if Rose followed him or not. She had to make her own decision.

On his way to the barn door, Flynn picked up a pitchfork from a nearby stack of hay. When he heard the rattle of someone opening the door from the inside, he quickened his pace and pressed his back to the wooden wall of the barn just next to the entrance. A second later, Rose caught up and moved next to him.

The tall form of Mistress emerged from the barn and she closed the door behind herself again.

Hatred drove away any pain Flynn felt in his wrists and hands. He gripped the shaft of the pitchfork tightly.

Mistress must have seen the empty cage, because her mouth fell wide open and she spun around to re-enter the barn. But she never made it. Flynn put all his effort into driving the sharp prongs of the tool up through the bottom of her chin.

The power Flynn drove the fork with forced two of the three prongs out of the top of Mistress' head with a wet crack. The impaling drove her tongue from her mouth and switched her off instantly.

As the large woman fell forward, Flynn let go of his tool, jumped aside, and watched both of them clatter into the barn's doors before they fell to the ground.

The sound called through the quiet complex and Flynn's heart beat double time. He stared at the barn door and waited for the people to rush out of it.

Chapter Seventy-One

About twenty seconds passed where Flynn stood waiting for the assault. But no one came out. They must have heard the noise. Maybe they assumed Mistress made it and there was nothing to worry about. He looked down at her slumped corpse.

Flynn pulled the fork out of Mistress. The spikes came free with a wet *schlop*. He wedged the weapon through the handles on the barn's doors and stepped back. It wouldn't hold them for long.

The trailer they'd taken from the community they last raided sat nearby. After Flynn had dragged Mistress' body away from the doors, he turned to Rose and said, "Come on," before running over to it.

Together, they moved the cart close to the barn, Flynn leading the way. He purposefully dragged it so it ran across the doors, but he'd left about a metre gap between the trailer and the barn.

"What are you doing?" Rose asked.

No time to explain, Flynn tilted the empty cart onto its side so it toppled against the barn. It made an almighty clatter, but fell so the flat bed of it lay flush with the barn's exit. The wheels pointed outwards, the top two still turning.

Out of breath from the effort of tipping the trailer, Flynn said, "It'll be much harder to get out with it like that. And it's the only exit from the barn."

The first bang clattered into the other side of the doors, and Flynn watched on with his heart in his mouth. Another loud bang and the cart still didn't budge.

A marching band of thuds on the other side and still the cart held. The people in the barn yelled and screamed. So many voices, Flynn couldn't make sense of any of them.

As he stood there with Rose next to him, Flynn ran a hand over the top of his head. "We have to do something more than this. Given time, they'll get out of there."

"Shouldn't we just run?" Rose said.

"We can't let the Queen walk away from this."

Rose bounced on the balls of her feet, clearly not convinced by Flynn's plan. "Then what shall we do?"

A look at the hay he'd taken the fork from, and Flynn said, "We need to stack that around the base of the barn."

Although Rose looked like she'd reply, she paused and followed Flynn's line of sight. He looked at the hut the community used to cook food in. It stood empty, a fire clearly still lit inside because smoke rose from the chimney.

Chapter Seventy-Two

The next five minutes seemed to last forever as Flynn and Rose moved several large mounds of hay around the base of the barn. Flynn's breaths came so quickly, he had to stop a couple of times to fend off the panic that rose inside him and threatened to choke him off. The people inside attacked the door with what sounded like everything they had.

They placed most of the hay on the cart, but Flynn made sure they laid it out all the way around the large wooden structure. He'd seen Rose's apprehension in her movements, but she helped nonetheless. "I don't expect you to start the fire, you know," he said. "I remember what you said about the Queen forcing you to burn your community, but it needs to be done, so I'll do it."

Rose nodded at him, but she didn't speak.

Slick with sweat, everything either aching or stinging, Flynn found a shovel, ran over to the kitchen's stove, and shovelled out a mound of white-hot wood from it. The tradition to make sure everyone ate together probably now seemed like a bad idea to the Queen inside.

The people in the barn continued to bang and shout. Maybe some of them didn't deserve this, but how could Flynn tell? Even if they weren't the Queen, they'd given her permission to behave in the way she had. They'd enjoyed her cruelty, and he'd seen them be equally as cruel. The world wouldn't mourn their passing.

It made it easier to follow through when Flynn listened to their panic turning into threats. The insults they'd thrown at them when they stoned them in the cage came flooding back.

As hard as Flynn listened, he couldn't hear the Queen. She probably wouldn't give him the satisfaction of making a sound.

Back at the barn's door, Flynn held the shovel over the stack of hay on the cart. Just before he dropped it on, he looked at Rose. Although she didn't say anything, she stared at the white-hot wood. A deep frown crushed her face as if she fended off the sadness of what she'd had to do in her old community.

For the next few seconds they stood like that before Flynn yelled out and threw the shovel with the burning wood away from him. "For fuck's sake. I want to do it. You know I want to do it. But—"

"Not everyone inside that barn deserves to die."

Flynn sank as he sighed.

A few short steps and Rose closed the distance between them, put her hand on Flynn's forearm, and stared at him. "You're a good man."

"By keeping those fucks in there alive?"

"Yes."

All the while they stood there, the people inside continued to scream and shout. Flynn finally said, "Come on. Let's get out of here."

Chapter Seventy-Three

Even after they'd walked for hours, the first signs of night dimming the summer sky around them, Flynn still looked behind to check for pursuers. "Do you think they've made it out yet?"

"I hope not," Rose said and looked behind too, the wind tossing her fine hair.

"And do you think the horses will be okay?" They'd set all of them loose before they'd left. Neither of them liked the idea of learning to ride.

"Yeah, the community needed the horses much more than the horses needed them."

Flynn turned back to where they'd been looking. Far enough away they wouldn't be seen, especially in amongst the long grass, but close enough for him to see the people clearly.

"It's like I was never there," Flynn said as he watched the residents of Home pack up for the day. When he saw Brian, Sharon, and Dan, he shook his head. "I hated those fuckers. See those three, the ones walking around like they own the place. They were the ones who killed Vicky."

Rose let him speak.

"Before I left, I tied each of them to their bed and gagged them. I pretended like I was going to kill them." Flynn smiled slightly at the thought. "To see Brian piss himself was enough. Killing him wouldn't bring Vicky back."

To watch Home now, Flynn said, "Maybe I had a lucky break." Then he saw Angelica. She walked through the place, holding hands with Larry. A bitter taste rose in his mouth for a moment, but he swallowed it down. Maybe she'd done him a favour. He might have stayed if she hadn't called it off.

A look at Rose and Flynn took in her natural beauty. A kind face and deep brown eyes, she had a wisdom well beyond either of their years. "It's only been a short time since I left," he said, "but I feel like Home was a lifetime ago. Like a different me lived there."

"But we're still going to risk our lives to save it?"

"I'm going to, yes," Flynn said. "I had a chance to kill the Queen and didn't take it. I can't walk away from that. I can't put all the innocent people in Home in danger, just like I couldn't kill the innocent people in the royal complex. You need to do what you think's right."

A sparkle in her brown eyes and she repeated, "But we're still going to risk our lives to save it." Before Flynn could reply, she laughed. "You're not going to get rid of me that easily."

Flynn couldn't help but smile. "I was hoping you'd say that. We'll be okay, won't we?"

A shrug, and Rose smiled. "We've been okay so far."

Flynn smiled too. "We have, haven't we?" He led the way in turning his back on Home. He didn't know what lay ahead of them. He didn't know whether they'd even survive against the Queen. But he knew what was right and he needed to follow that. Thankfully, he'd have Rose beside him.

Ends.

Would you like to be notified when I have new books and special offers? Join my mailing list for all of my updates here:

www.michaelrobertson.co.uk

Support the Author

Dear reader, as an independent author I don't have the resources of a huge publisher. If you like my work and would like to see more from me in the future, there are two things you can do to help: leaving a review, and a word-of-mouth referral.

Releasing a book takes many hours and hundreds of dollars. I love to write, and would love to continue to do so. All I ask is that you leave an Amazon review. It shows other readers that you've enjoyed the book and will encourage them to give it a try too. The review can be just one sentence, or as long as you like.

Other Works Available by Michael Robertson

The Shadow Order - Available Now:

New Reality: Truth - Available now for FREE:

Crash - Available now for FREE:

Rat Run - Available Now:

For my other titles and mailing list - go to
www.michaelrobertson.co.uk

About The Author

Like most children born in the seventies, Michael grew up with Star Wars, Aliens, and George Romero in his life. An obsessive watcher of movies, and an avid reader from an early age, he found himself taken over with stories whenever he let his mind wander.

Those stories had to come out.

He hopes you enjoy reading his books as much as he does writing them.

Michael loves to travel when he can. He has a young family, who are his world, and when he's not reading, he enjoys walking so he can dream up more stories.

To be notified of Michael's future books, please sign up at www.michaelrobertson.co.uk

Email at: subscribers@michaelrobertson.co.uk

Follow me on facebook at –
https://www.facebook.com/MichaelRobertsonAuthor

Twitter at – @MicRobertson

Google Plus at –
https://plus.google.com/u/0/113009673177382863155/posts

SIXTH CYCLE

Nuclear war has destroyed human civilization.
Captain Jake Phillips wakes into a dangerous new world, where he finds the remaining fragments of the population living in a series of strongholds, connected across the country. Uneasy alliances have maintained their safety, but things are about to change. — Discovery **leads to danger.** — Skye Reed, a tracker from the Omega stronghold, uncovers a threat that could spell the end for their fragile society. With friends and enemies revealing truths about the past, she will need to decide who to trust. — **Sixth Cycle** is a gritty post-apocalyptic story of survival and adventure.

Darren Wearmouth ~ Carl Sinclair

DEAD ISLAND: Operation Zulu

Ten years after the world was nearly brought to its knees by a zombie Armageddon, there is a race for the antidote! On a remote Caribbean island, surrounded by a horde of hungry living dead, a team of American and Australian commandos must rescue the Antidotes' scientist. Filled with zombies, guns, Russian bad guys, shady government types, serial killers and elevator muzak. Dead Island is an action packed blood soaked horror adventure.

Allen Gamboa

INVASION OF THE DEAD SERIES

This is the first book in a series of nine, about an ordinary bunch of friends, and their plight to survive an apocalypse in Australia. — Deep beneath defense headquarters in the Australian Capital Territory, the last ranking Army chief and a brilliant scientist struggle with answers to the collapse of the world, and the aftermath of an unprecedented virus. Is it a natural mutation, or does the infection contain — more sinister roots? — One hundred and fifty miles away, five friends returning from a month-long camping trip slowly discover that death has swept through the country. What greets them in a gradual revelation is an enemy beyond compare. — Armed with dwindling ammunition, the friends must overcome their disagreements, utilize their individual skills, and face unimaginable horrors as they battle to reach their hometown…

Owen Baillie

WHISKEY TANGO FOXTROT

Alone in a foreign land. The radio goes quiet while on convoy in Afghanistan, a lost patrol alone in the desert. With his unit and his home base destroyed, Staff Sergeant Brad Thompson suddenly finds himself isolated and in command of a small group of men trying to survive in the Afghan wasteland. **Every turn leads to danger**

The local population has been afflicted with an illness that turns them into rabid animals. They pursue him and his men at every corner and stop. Struggling to hold his team together and unite survivors, he must fight and evade his way to safety.

A fast paced zombie war story like no other.

W.J. Lundy

ZOMBIE RUSH

New to the Hot Springs PD Lisa Reynolds was not all that welcomed by her coworkers especially those who were passed over for the position. It didn't matter, her thirty days probation ended on the same day of the Z-poc's arrival. Overnight the world goes from bad to worse as thousands die in the initial onslaught. National Guard and regular military unit deployed the day before to the north leaves the city in mayhem. All directions lead to death until one unlikely candidate steps forward with a plan. A plan that became an avalanche raging down the mountain culminating in the salvation or destruction of them all.

Joseph Hansen

THE ALPHA PLAGUE

Rhys is an average guy who works an average job in Summit City—a purpose built government complex on the outskirts of London. The Alpha Tower stands in the centre of the city. An enigma, nobody knows what happens behind its dark glass. Rhys is about to find out. At ground zero and with chaos spilling out into the street, Rhys has the slightest of head starts. If he can remain ahead of the pandemonium, then maybe he can get to his loved ones before the plague does. The Alpha Plague is a post-apocalyptic survival thriller.

Michael Robertson

THE GATHERING HORDE

The most ambitious terrorist plot ever undertaken is about to be put into motion, releasing an unstoppable force against humanity. Ordinary people – A group of students celebrating the end of the semester, suburban and rural families – are about to themselves in the center of something that threatens the survival of the human species. As they battle the dead – and the living – it's going to take every bit of skill, knowledge and luck for them to survive in Zed's World.

Rich Baker

THE RECKONING
Australia has been invaded.

While the outnumbered Australian Defence Force fights on the ground, in the air and at sea, this quickly becomes a war involving ordinary people. Ben, an IT consultant has never fought a day in his life. Will he survive? Grant, a security guard at Sydney's International Airport, finds himself captured and living in the filth and squalor of one of the concentration camps dotted around Australia. Knowing death awaits him if he stays, he plans a daring escape. This is a dark day in Australia's history. This is terror, loneliness, starvation and adrenaline all mixed together in a sour cocktail. This is the day Australia fell.

Keith McArdle

GRUDGE

The United States Navy led an expedition to Antarctica in December 1946, called Operation Highjump. Officially, the men were tasked with evaluating the effect of cold weather on US equipment; secretly their mission was to investigate reports of a hidden Nazi base buried beneath the ice. After engaging unknown forces in aerial combat, weather forced the Navy to abandon operations. Undeterred, the US returned every Antarctic summer until finally the government detonated three nuclear missiles over the atmosphere in 1958. Unfortunately, the desperate gamble to rid the world of the Nazi scourge failed.

The enemy burrowed deeper into the ice, using alien technologies for cryogenic freezing to amass a genetically superior army, indoctrinated from birth to hate Americans.

Now they've returned, intent on exacting revenge for the destruction of their homeland and banishment to the icy wastes.

Brian Parker

<<<<>>>>

Made in the USA
Columbia, SC
02 December 2020